THE PROVIDENT
EVENTS

ISBN-13   Paperback   978-1-967903-68-9
           eBook   978-1-967903-69-6

Library of Congress Control Number: 2025916769

THE PROVIDENT EVENTS

RAN DOLPH POOLE

For My Brother, Elgin

Continued Rest in Eternal Peace

SYNOPSIS

J ace Coffey's life is in turmoil. His wife is angry. He has few friends. His job hangs in the balance. He meets and finds an empathetic ear in Perry St. Kane, an unexpected lifeline, who, too, grapples with his own personal calamities. The two, brought together by circumstance, build a lasting friendship. Jace is plagued by unpleasant events in his life and Perry is always there to lend support and reassurance. By coincidence, they become roommates. Jace's world is further rocked when his family becomes the target of unscrupulous activity, even the threat of death; and he again finds comfort in Perry. But Perry's loyalty masks a deeper truth—one he fears could destroy the very friendship he cherishes. Revelations are met with consequences when the two friends unexpectedly find themselves caught in conditions far beyond their control.

"A compelling, must-read anecdote of unrequited love, taboo relationships, and betrayal."

PREFACE

Dear Readers:

The Provident Events is my first foray in the book-writing arena. What an experience it has been—laborious and exhaustive, yet joyous and rewarding. Allow me to transport you away from the sometimes drudgery of life, to another place, a simpler time, and new acquaintances.

Meet Perry St. Kane. Travel with him to Provident Falls, home to the Coffey family. Good people, *in grave danger*.

It is Christmastime, circa 2002. The tree has been trimmed. Gifts have been purchased. A table has been spread. Death lurks in the shadows—Waiting.

Enjoy the ride.

— Ran

CONTENTS

PROLOGUE

I t was a cold and sunny Christmas morning, the perfect day for a road trip. Two friends, Jace Coffey and Perry St. Kane, traveled northeast on US Highway 59 in the southernmost part of the state, winding their way across the scenic countryside of the two-lane asphalt road, divided by yellow center striping. Perry, the older of the two, was in the drivers' seat. It was not the most direct route but offered more of a visual feast over the much faster, although quite bland and boring interstate system. They were in no big hurry, allowing for plenty of time to revel in the breath-taking views of the towering mountains and woodland countryside—picturesque scenes worthy of a Hallmark greeting card. It was bitterly cold outside with a light dusting of 'powder' over the panoramic landscape. Protected from the frigid temperatures inside the warm and cozy comfort of the sports car, the two friends sung joyfully along to some of the holiday classics being played on the radio. Jace sat in the passenger seat madly conducting an imaginary orchestra and choir to the seasonal favorite tune of *Carol of the Bells* that was being given the airtime. He increased the volume, filling the car with the melodious sound from its eight-way stereo speaker system. His maestro mannerisms continued, becoming more pronounced and direct as he brought his palms together, faced them forward, then pulled them back toward his chest, with a slight left turn of his head and furrowing of his eyebrows to signal the tenor section of the imaginary ensemble to *pianissimo* or sing very softly. The song ended with a roar of cheer and applause from the radio audience. Jace, still in conductor mode, nodded his head in an obligatory *thank you,* while simultaneously extending his arm back in recognition of the nonexistent chorus members. Perry chuckled at his exaggerated directorial display. The car zipped past a mileage sign that read Provident Falls 25. They were only thirty minutes away from their destination—Jace's parents' home. After an encore radio performance of *Bells*, Jace gave Perry directives for their holiday stay at his parents' place. Unfolding drama was common at the Coffey house and for that reason Perry liked to have advance warning of what to expect. Visits to the home were usually pre-empted by a set of rules governing one's actions based on the activities of the day.

"Just mind the trains," Jace ordered. "And don't pet the dog."

"Very well," Perry acknowledged at his behest.

"And for Heaven's sake, don't encourage my dad," Jace further instructed. There had been an incident with the dog leaving him in stitches and still very sore. The slightest touch would send the canine yelping in pain and protest as if Death itself were in the very room and ready to take the furry friend at any moment. The commotion was enough to send the entire household into a frenzy, with particular upset to Mr. Coffey; hence, the no petting order. The trains were a prized possession of the elder Coffey, whose delight in them was woefully tolerated. To maintain the harmony of any social gathering with him in attendance, it was best he not become agitated or excitable. He hadn't always been this way. They passed the city limit sign of Provident Falls and within five minutes were in the driveway of Jace's parents' home just on the outskirts of town. It was considerably colder with a heavier coating of snow. His mother's poinsettias at the front door were bursting with deep, rich, red color and thrived in the chilly temperatures. The family cat sat in the foyer window on guard duty—by her own right—and peered out at them suspiciously through the condensation of the windowpanes, her face distorted by the beading water droplets and streaks. Perry rung the bell and could hear its eight-tone alert chime from inside the house. Moments later the door opened to Mr. Coffey standing there, disheveled and grinning, and staring at them impatiently as though they were about to give him an unsolicited sales pitch of some product or service that was not wanted. *Invite us in, cuckoo. It's cold out here.* They had arrived.

PART ONE

CHAPTER ONE

A Christmas Gathering

Perry sat in an oversized and overstuffed leather chair and watched him. Jace lay comfortably on the matching sleeper sofa resting peacefully, as peaceful as a newborn baby. Perry watched him.

Snow had fallen during the night. Thick whiteness enveloped the landscape of Jace's parents' ranch-style home, clinging to naked magnolia trees as if protecting them from the winter element. The serenity of such a sight was paralleled only by that of the incredible being that lay before him, Perry thought, tranquility as soothing as the uninterrupted snow. A man of thirty years, Jace lay there completely oblivious to his audience of one. At five-feet-ten inches tall, he was a few inches shorter than Perry. His tousled dirty-blonde hair had a charm all its own, well on its way to becoming a waterfall of wonder cascading over his shoulders and down his back. He had hypnotic blue-grey eyes that contrasted against his pallid face, separated by a narrow nose. His lips, though thin, held a supple inviting. There he lay. Perry counted each breath as though it were Jace's last and recorded his slightest movement as if watching a high-wire acrobat. He sat watching, lost in a world of fantasy and longing. Then, as quickly as the morning sun began to melt the snow from its home on the magnolia branches and send it thrashing to the ground, he was suddenly reminded of Jace's date with *her* on Sunday.

Jace Coffey and Perry St. Kane shared an apartment. They hadn't known each other very long at all when they signed the one-year rental agreement some five months earlier. It seemed a bit out of the ordinary that two complete strangers would find themselves rooming together in such a short time of being acquainted, but they did. Christmas Day had arrived. They were spending it with Jace's family in Provident Falls. Perry, whose family lived in another state, was feeling aloof over the holiday season. Jace was kind enough to invite him to spend it with his. Perry graciously accepted. Mrs. Coffey, whom he had met before, was a gentle woman and took him as her own. Twin brothers with their respective girlfriends would be joining them from nearby Common Wells. Mr. Coffey, a jolly, robust fellow of fifty-seven years, had a hearing deficit and wore an aid; without it, you may as well have been talking to yourself. He would never hear. A congenital defect rendered him near deaf. He shared an affinity of model trains and made certain everybody knew it. Greeting them at the door, disheveled and grinning, he wore his customary striped conductors cap with accompanying coveralls supporting his plump belly. He gave Perry a firm slap on the back that sent him stumbling into the foyer. Evidence of Mr. Coffey's preoccupation with model trains was everywhere as one rattled past them from above. Radius, the yellow lab, had been forever banished to the backyard because of a recent derailment at his expense. Maylay, the tabby, stayed clear of the mechanical madness.

"How was the drive?" Mr. Coffey asked them, while watching the power-driven train make yet another revolution as if for the very first time. Jace rolled his eyes.

"Fine," they both declared in unison, their response falling on deaf ears as Mr. Coffey was now bent over inspecting the train's caboose. The delightful aroma of baked goods wafted through the house. They made their way to the kitchen.

Mrs. Coffey, Trudy, as she is known, was at war with dinner in the kitchen and appeared to be losing. Her head well into the oven, she did not hear them come in. Judging by the chaos of the kitchen, the turkey had won the fight. She emerged from the oven with mitten hands holding a pumpkin pie—Perry's favorite; she knew he was coming. Nearly dropping the pie from excitement at seeing them, she slammed it on the counter and embraced them both, one under each arm. Perry was more concerned with the well-being of the pie.

"Is there anything we can do to help?" he chuckled, looking around at the melee of the kitchen.

"Call out for pizza," she quipped.

Pizza and pumpkin pie, Perry thought; *now there's an interesting combination.*

There would be no ordering of pizza. She was an excellent cook. This battle would be decided at the dinner table.

"How's your family?" she asked him.

"Just great," Perry gleefully feigned. He hadn't spoken to them in months.

"Praise God!" she replied, as every answer in the positive realm was met with this enthusiastic response from her. She wasn't as holy as one might be led to believe, lest her enthusiastic 'Praise God!' be misconstrued.

On occasion, an expletive would slip from her tongue, much to her own chagrin and the amusement of others.

"Amen!" Perry replied in acknowledgement, and to also end the discussion of his family.

His mother died the day after Christmas, thirty years ago. He was only three years old. She was twenty-six.

Her untimely death invariably led to his detachment during the Christmas time of year. He hastily brought any hint of conversation regarding it to an abrupt end. Mrs. Coffey did not press further. She offered them a drink. Perry helped himself to a refreshing glass of iced tea, handing Jace a glass as well while he inspected the contents of various sized simmering pots atop the stove. The pride and joy of the Christmas dinner would be his mother's dressing, with just the right blending of ingredients to satisfy even the most fastidious palate.

It had won awards, been featured in some of the better-known cookbooks, and was a source of contention at the annual state fair cook-off. For three consecutive years, it had captured the coveted and prized blue ribbon, to the dismay of her rivals. Townspeople joked of her being kidnapped and held hostage, then made to talk, revealing the secret of her winning recipe. Mrs. Coffey had little time for the amateurs and wannabes. Her sights were set on the ultimate in prize bestowal and recognition, a place in the crème de la crème of homemaking magazines, *Better Homes & Gardens* and *Southern Living*, in that order. One more blue ribbon and they'd come a 'calling. She was sure of it. She had reached celebrity status for her turkey and dressing locally. Jace would make it a point of returning home with a care package of the delectable dish. She paused for a moment from her busying about the kitchen to assess the integrity of the aforementioned pie. Jace continued his investigation of the dinner offerings atop and in the stove. Perry sat on a bar stool at the center island of the kitchen sipping the iced tea. They could hear the whistle and rattle of the model train from the foyer. Jace turned to his mother and asked, "How long has he been at it this time?"

"For the better part of the day," she replied, referencing her husband and the trains.

"Just as I thought. Those trains are going to be the death of him yet," he said wittingly.

"Jace!" she rebuked. "It's your father's only stronghold since the accident. Let him have his fun. Plus, it keeps him out of my hair."

"Sure mom, after all, you *were* the one who started it." Mr. Coffey could be heard muttering to himself in the other room, his speech incomprehensible.

The doorbell rang announcing the arrival of the twins, Alex and Asher, and their girlfriends. It would be Perry's first time meeting the brothers. They were perfect clones of one another. Only a mother could tell them apart. Handsome men, they were in stark contrast to their elder sibling. One was a musician, the other an aspiring actor. From the foyer they heard Mr. Coffey yell back to them in proclamation, "A BOVINE IN A DRESS!" This reference was made to Jessyca, Alex's girl. She took no offense considering the source. Trudy appeared from the kitchen to chasten her husband and silence the outburst. Rebuked, he returned to his trains. Asher's girlfriend, Kali, was a vision and exuded confidence and congeniality. Her shoulders-length, golden brown hair accentuated her perfectly oval face. She spoke softly and carried herself with the grace of a parochial school alum. Jessyca, in contrast, was a portly being, loud and boisterous, and lumbered about with much effort. The two were complete opposites of one another. Jace hinted of tension between them.

The stage was set. All the players were present and accounted for, having traveled from various origins. The model train continued its endless journey around the house, unnerving Jace. Mr. Coffey again made references to herd and cattle, with random outbursts of cow moos and elephant cries, directed at Jessyca. Trudy's orchestra of pots and pans clanging together played on from the kitchen. Asher and Kali continued a heated argument, which they had on the drive over, while Alex took over as disciplinarian of his father. Perry took his glass of tea to the enclosed back porch to see Radius. The dog was spread out lazily on the floor. He raised his head up briefly to acknowledge Perry and then resumed his lazy lounging. Maylay snubbed the gathered assembly and meandered about the house checking the various rooms and under furniture for any unauthorized visitors. It would make for an interesting holiday gathering.

CHAPTER TWO

In The Beginning

The attraction wasn't immediate, at first. Nonexistent almost. Jace was not one to turn heads upon entering a room but did have an appealing quality that proved hard for Perry to resist. Through the course of them rooming together a bond was building stronger than they could have imagined, albeit one-sided, Perry's.

It was summertime, earlier that year. Perry was sitting at a desk in the reception area of his employer. He was only able to see legs as they approached the front entrance from the outside. Horizontal blinds were half drawn over the glass doors blocking a full view. His office was in the rear of the building; the copier is what brought him to the front. Once completing his copies, he lingered in the reception area engaged in some trivial task, while waiting to see who was attached to the remarkable set of quads and calves and to be the one to help with the query. The door chime sounded alerting the office staff to a visitor. At the same time Perry had arisen with the false pretense of heading back to his office when Jace entered. Perry greeted him and offered assistance. The receptionist continued her data entry. Jace, already employed with the company, was transferring to the Royalton office, and had been sent by corporate to complete some essential HR-related tasks prior to starting. Because Jace was a current employee, there would be no need for a background check or drug screen; just a routine performance review from the corporate offices in Sheffield.

Perry delighted in the knowledge. They exchanged prolonged glances. Perry offered a warm smile. Jace returned the same.

"I'm sorry, I didn't catch your name," Perry said to him.

"Jace," he replied. "Jace Coffey." Perry made a mental note. Extending a hand, Perry introduced himself, "I'm Perry. Perry St. Kane." They shook, their hands staying firmly locked for a delayed second before release. After a moment of awkward silence, Perry finally interjected, "Well, good luck," before heading down the hall. Because of his tenure with the company, and clout, he would make sure it was a successful transfer.

The twins had heard all about Perry from their big brother. That was encouraging to him, considering he and Jace had only known each other a short while. Perry, too, had dabbled in the theater and that was of particular interest to Asher, the actor. They shared stories of plays, auditions, callbacks, and the like.

Asher was soon to audition for a small part in an upcoming television special. Perry wished him well.

More on his mind was what Jace had said about him to the family. Acquiring that information would require some skillful probing, but to Perry's surprise, it was offered. There seemed to be some concern on the twins' part about the mental well-being of their older sibling. With a marriage teetering on divorce and instability at work, Jace had become somewhat of a recluse, distancing himself from family and what few friends he had. He had bouts of depression that concerned them and was a reluctant voice of his feelings.

At times, weeks would go by without any communication from him or even a simple return of the brother's phone calls. It wasn't until he met Perry that his behavior began to change, and for the better. The family seemed relieved at Jace's sudden interest in his newfound friendship and took a special liking to Perry because of it. Perry was happy to oblige. Had Trudy plotted their meeting and conversation to reinforce his continued involvement in her son's life? He wondered.

"Jace thinks you're a pretty cool guy," Alex began.

"Oh?" Perry responded, suggesting elaboration.

"Yeah, he's pretty excited about livin' with ya." *Tell me more,* Perry thought.

"Coming from him, that says a lot. He doesn't get close to very many people," Alex concluded.

"You're a celebrity of sorts as far as he's concerned," Jessyca added. "Perry this and Perry that," she continued.

"Says he's even inspired to work out if his body could look like yours," Asher chimed in. *He'd taken notice. A few months in the gym would do him good indeed,* Perry determined. Not knowing what to say, he simply smiled. Kali offered no input. Instead, logged an entry into a kept journal and dazed out the window. Few things happened without escaping the pages of her diary. It went everywhere with her, a veritable camcorder in book form. Oh, the telling stories it held captive beyond its locked jacket.

Unbeknownst to him and because of Perry, Jace Coffey began working out of the Royalton office the following week. The report back from corporate on him was not favorable. Excessive tardiness. Absenteeism. Documentation errors. Poor attitude. Even his appearance. Defending the less-than-flattering report proved almost hopeless without knowing anything of his character. Perry turned out to be his lone advocate on a panel of seven review peers. Ultimately, they acquiesced and decided Perry would be the one to orient Jace on their office way of doing things. Jace was happy to see a familiar face. An "at-will" employee, he could be terminated at any time for any reason or none at all. One slip-up and he would be gone. Perry was determined not to let that happen and took him under his wing. He would later share this information with Jace in hopes of winning his favor.

Orientation was a matter of going over the ins and outs, and dos and don'ts of the Royalton office. Each branch was its own entity and operated independently of the others. It was lunchtime. They decided to take a break and grab a bite to eat. Perry saw it as an opportunity to become more familiar with their new employee.

"So what brings you to Royalton?" He asked Jace, over a bowl of pasta and Caesar salad.

"Needed a change," Jace answered.

"How so?"

"My wife," Jace stated unenthusiastically.

"Oh, so you're marri—," Perry started to ask.

"—Separated," Jace interrupted, then added, "We still live together though."

"Any kids?" Perry continued. Silence. "Listen, if I'm getting too personal…"

"No, no, it's ok really," Jace replied. "We tried counseling. It didn't help. It's pretty much a done deal. After six years, she wants out; filed papers the same day I came into the office, last week."

"Man, I'm so sorry," Perry offered, though not really, and not sure of what else to say.

"It's probably for the best," Jace stated, somewhat distant and defeated. "No kids."

"You okay?" Perry asked him.

"Yeah, I'll be alright, thanks."

"No problem," Perry reassured him. "If you need to talk…"

Jace smiled at him and said, "I just might need to, you got a number?"

Perry took out a business card and wrote his number and personal e-mail on the back then slid it across the table. Jace examined the front of the card. *St. Kane*, he read.

"You're Irish?" he asked Perry, as if it were not possible for him to be.

"Part Irish," Perry laughed. "My dad is Irish; my mother was black."

"*Was?*" Jace questioned.

"She's dead," Perry informed, with reservation, and in a manner as to dissuade further questioning of the revelation. Jace took the card and stuffed it in his wallet. It was nearing two o'clock and they needed to get back to the office. Perry picked up the tab for lunch. They headed back in Jace's cramped sports car, which he was as fond of as the senior Coffey was of his trains set.

The return conversation was more relaxed with them having developed a comfort level with each other. Jace even opened up a bit, sharing some things that were probably more reserved for a close friend or relative. Perry listened intently as Jace detailed the events that set his marriage on its spiraling course of end. As it turns out, Mrs. Jace Coffey had come forth with a confession, rather *confessions,* of infidelity, sighting him not *being there* for her as the cause. Struggling to make ends meet, he had taken on a second job all so she could have a better life. The trade-off would mean late nights away from home. She had been accustomed to the finer things in life, but at the expense of someone else; her finances were bleak, at best. He worked overtime to support her discriminating tastes. Irritability and fatigue were taking their toll on the marriage. Their fights were more frequent and threatened to become physical. Already sleeping in separate rooms, their conversations were out of necessity only. No good mornings. No good nights. Dinner was a solitary event. To add insult to injury, the 'other' man was a mutual friend they both had confided in. Jace, subsequently, had a disdain for the institution of marriage and vowed never to again. Perry offered what condolences he could. Jace seemed relieved at just being able to talk about it. She would get the furniture, fanciful artwork, kitchen appliances, and most of the electronics. He would be left with an alarm clock, a pet boa constrictor, and a ferret. "*Weasel,*" Perry called it, to Jace's objection.

Perry concluded that Jace's par performance at work stemmed from the separation and eventual divorce. Coupled with the strain of financial burden and it was the recipe for his poor review from the corporate office. Understandable, he reasoned. Having this information gave him ammunition for defense of Jace, if needed. They rode along listening to the radio. After a song, Perry asked him, "You commuting from Sheffield every day?"

"For the time being, yes," Jace answered. "I'm looking for a place. Got any suggestions?"

"Stay away from the west side," Perry warned. "I'm in the market for a new place myself," he added, which wasn't entirely true. His lease wouldn't expire for another three months. It was bait. Jace didn't bite.

Instead, they decided to go on an apartment-hunting quest together. It would be to Jace's advantage, being new to the area;

to Perry's advantage, securing another outing with Jace. With the radio now blaring out a chorus of *The Things We Do for Love*, they decided Saturday would be the day.

They arrived back at the office. At six-foot-one, exiting the car required some agility and clever contortion. Perry twisted himself out. Jace grabbed his arm and stopped him just outside the front entrance. "Thanks for the ear," he said in earnest. Perry sensed a yearning in his voice, a longing in his face, the need for a friend. Intuitively, he knew that Jace had enjoyed his company. The feeling was mutual. It would be the establishment of a resilient bond that would build between the two of them. He looked back at him and replied, "Hey, anytime," then placed an arm around Jace's shoulders and gave him an encouraging hug.

Jace reciprocated in like manner. They embraced.

CHAPTER THREE

The Behemoth

On a stormy autumn day of that same year, Mr. Coffey left his office on the ninth floor of the mid-rise building where he worked. It was a late Friday evening. He was not alone. As a prominent business attorney, he was well respected in the Provident Falls community. Earlier that year, he had taken on a formidable chemical refining company, Titan/Hutt Industries, Inc., from building a processing plant in their fair city and had become somewhat of a local hero because of it. That day, looming tragedy hovered over him. Death lay in wait as a cobra ready to strike. The 'accident,' as Trudy liked to refer to it, left his once brilliant mind relegated to a world of daydreaming and simplicity. To this day his experience remains an inexplicable event shrouded in mystery. Only he held the key to unlock the answers. His mind reduced to that of a child offered little hope of ever solving the mysterious happenings of that late Friday evening.

He was a ruthless attorney who had gone up against such forces as organized crime and big industry, with similar cases pending. It was suspected he had become a target because of the refinery case. At stake were large sums of money to be profited by Titan/Hutt with the plant being built in the Falls community. He ruined all chances of that for the giant corporation with a unanimous jury siding in his favor. Titan/Hutt executives were outraged and vowed a vicious appeal, losing once again. They despised his repeated successful efforts against them but were tenacious in their resolve. Rumor had it the attorney was considering a council seat run in the district of the proposed plant. If so, and if elected, the revenue-generating project for Titan/Hutt would be in grave danger of almost certain defeat. With virtually no one to oppose him in an election, it was a distinct possibility. Titan/Hutt officials were notably concerned and scrambled to plot a strategy. They had friends and contacts in the judicial system but were in hostile territory here. Mr. Coffey was a favorite among the county judges and had a strong backing of the local community. They loved him.

Titan/Hutt Industries, Inc. was a multi-billion-dollar behemoth, publicly traded, with interests in everything from household goods to environmental conservatories. It was a feared adversary in the business community, and operated in the black but under the watchful eye and close scrutiny of federal authorities. Its books were 'fixed' to hide some of its more lucrative and shady dealings. It dealt business with countries all over the world, so it seemed unlikely that an unassuming Falls community could hinder one of its most profitable endeavors, but it had, and at the helm, was the attorney. They loathed him. Some of the locals suspected Mafia involvement. Attorney Donerson Eugene Coffey needed to be silenced; it was ominously feared. Anonymous phone calls rang into his office, spoken all in angry pig Latin. Threats arrived in the guise of flower bouquets, thank you cards, sweet treats, and the like. They had not yet reached his home on Galatian Avenue. Trudy was not privy to the happenings. He didn't want to alarm her. Mr. Coffey refused police and guard protection. He found solace in their small suburban community of Provident Falls, Texas – a mistake.

Mrs. Coffey was home alone.

It was one of many nights he would be working late. Sitting at the breakfast table, she was preparing activities for a local Youth House, where she volunteered working with at-risk and disadvantaged teens. Radius trotted over to announce his need for a bathroom break and frivolity in the backyard. She let him out. Back inside, she went into the kitchen to make a pot of coffee. Looking out the window above the sink, she saw the dog frolicking with one of his playthings and smiled to herself at his romping about. Maylay perched herself in the breakfast nook bay window to watch the ridiculous display from the canine. Having had enough, she raised herself and jumped down from the window to make her rounds of the house. Nothing had changed since her last survey twenty minutes ago. Everything in order, she returned to the bay window and assumed her previous position. She cocked her head for signs of the dog. Not seeing him from that vantage point, she tipped into the kitchen and leapt onto the counter at the sink. She intensely stared out the window but with no sighting of Radius. She had grown up with the dog since a kitten and he a pup, and although she detested him, he was her ride or die. A sense of foreboding overcame the feline, and she alerted Trudy with repeated meows and head gestures as if to say, 'Look at what I *don't* see.' Trudy petted her and continued with the coffee making. Maylay, wide-eyed and still staring hard, spotted movement in the outside darkness. A dark silhouette figure, unlike that of a dog, darted past the kitchen window. She quickly followed suit. Her meows became more intense and then fell quiet. An eerie silence filled the house. Maylay was on heightened alert, with no movement or sound escaping her. Her body tensed as she went into attack mode, ready to pounce whatever lay in wait. The distant sound of a ticking clock was heard. The Coffey residence did not house any audible clocks, ticking or otherwise. Trudy, hearing the noise, went to investigate. Upon seeing Maylay erect and poised, she became alarmed. The coffeepot whistled its readiness breaking the ticking silence. Startled, Trudy gasped and jumped simultaneously, then retreated to the kitchen. She grabbed the handle to remove the pot from the burner and quiet the whistling. Shattering glass resonated the house from the breakfast nook.

In concert, Trudy dropped the hot pot of coffee on the ceramic-tiled floor. She hurried to the breakfast nook.

Radius lay whimpering on the floor with shards of glass impaled in his back. He had been hurled through the window. Hysterical, she called Eugene.

The police arrived at the home to find a dazed Mrs. Coffey. Mr. Coffey arrived shortly thereafter. Her leg had been scalded. An ambulance was summoned. Radius, still whimpering, was taken away to the vet. He would be okay but would require numerous sutures. She sustained a first-degree burn to the foot and was given a cold compress to relieve the pain and reduce any swelling. It would not require any further medical attention. Maylay pranced over to her. *I tried to tell you*, she seemed to communicate before waltzing off.

The day of reckoning had come for Mr. Coffey. Trudy was disappointed he had not informed her of the threats. Their lives were in potential danger, and he had decided not to disclose this to her. She went cold.

Terror had reached the home on Galatian Avenue. Their solace had been silenced.

Mr. Coffey found himself in the eleven-story parking garage of his downtown office building. Parked on level ten, his office was on the ninth floor. It was well after hours, nearing midnight. He had been working late preparing a case. Once exiting from the main building after hours, reentry was not allowed. Upon reaching the tenth level parking, *his* was the only car in sight. Security made their rounds hourly. Willie, the night shift security guard, stopped and chatted with him before getting into the golf cart with the blue beacon on top to begin his hourly rounds of the parking garage. It was the eleven o'clock hour when he waved the attorney goodbye and hobbled off in the motorized cart. As Mr. Coffey walked to his car, he saw no reason for flashes of shadowy figures to appear on the walls of the parking garage, but there they were, in a fanciful dance of courtship and torment. He dismissed them as activity from the outside. Forecasters had predicted thunderstorms with torrential rains. Inclement weather threatened to disrupt the quiet evening.

He had had battery problems before and knew that a new one was imminent. Another crank of the ignition, his car would not start. Calling from his cellular phone, the pleasant and soothing voice of the recording informed: *We're sorry, all circuits are busy now; will you please hang up and try your call again.* He did.

Your call cannot be completed as dialed; will you please hang up and try your call again, it repeated.

Exiting the car, he made his way toward the elevator. He pushed the down arrow of the elevator. It did not illuminate. Waiting, he made another attempt at the cell phone. *The number you have dialed has been disconnected. Please check the number and try your call again,* the recording informed. He pushed "0" on the phone for the operator. The pleasant voice returned: *We're sorry, all circuits are busy now; will you please hang up and try your call again.* A repeated push of the down arrow. The elevator did not open.

Returning to the car, he removed his tweed blazer and paisley tie for the ten-flight descent to ground level.

Locking the car doors behind him, he headed for the stairwell, where Death had made its temporary home.

CHAPTER FOUR

Oh Happy Day

Jace arrived at Perry's apartment early that Saturday summer morning. Perry, suddenly regretful of the apartment-hunting notion, suggested a quick stop for breakfast before their exhaustive search began. Jace agreed. Apartment hunting was low on their priority list of things to do, but a necessary evil for Jace being new to the area, though Perry's motive being ulterior. They stopped at a family-owned restaurant, called *Slap Your Mama*. A weathered sign dangled from an awning near the entrance and proudly warned: *Food so good, you'll Slap Your Mama*. They decided to investigate this claim. Once inside, they were greeted and seated promptly with a smile from Katina. Jace insisted on a booth by the window. A larger-than-life mural of The Last Supper occupied an entire wall in the restaurant, as Jesus and his disciples hovered over the diners in monumental style, like some gigantic statue of a founding forefather outside a government building. It was an establishment deeply rooted in religion and the church, as indicated not only by the massive mural, but also by the explosive gospel tunes being belted from the ceiling speakers. One might think a one hundred-voice choir was housed in the kitchen and that a revival would break out at any moment. A notable scripture was transcribed at the bottom of each menu. It was a feel-good kind of a place, and they did. They had a varying of opinions on religion, but for the most part, shared the same philosophies. Perry was reminded of an English term paper he had due his freshman year in college on the very topic, where his research would take him to a Pentecostal church and a firsthand account of one of its worship services. His experience there was a fascinating one, and one that Jace was anxious to hear about. Perry promised to expound at another time.

The uplifting and toe-tapping tune of *Oh Happy Day* came across the speakers, transporting them back to the days of that 'old time religion.' They sung joyfully along with the Edwin Hawkins gospel classic.

Regardless of one's religious affiliation, the old favorite would ring familiar in the ear of just about anyone and bring to memory its inspiring words of even the most ardent forgetful, the National Anthem of Christianity, Perry called it. Jace, having taken a liking to the place, decided he would invite his parents down and treat them to breakfast. A cup of coffee, black, for him, and a glass of orange juice, no ice, for Perry, soon arrived. He would have the flapjacks, as the menu read, with bacon. Jace decided on the house favorite of smoked shrimp and grits, with a side of fried potatoes. Water was complimentary.

"How was your evening?" Perry asked him, while they waited for their food.

"Same ole, same ole," Jace answered.

"What, another fight with the Mrs.?"

"How'd you guess?"

"Your cheek is still very red. Must've been a pretty powerful smack."

"Happened this morning, actually," Jace informed.

"Ouch!" Perry grimaced.

"Try being on the receiving end of one."

"I'll pass," Perry stated. "What did you do, *or say*, to justify it?" Jace did not answer him.

Dipping a folded napkin into the glass of iced water, Perry handed it to him to place over the offended cheek. The divorce could not come soon enough. Katina arrived with their food, fresh and piping hot.

"Will there be anything else?" she asked them.

"No," they said and thanked her. Refilling their drinks, she smiled and tipped away. Where food is concerned, presentation is everything. Theirs almost needed an introduction. It looked as though it came off the pages of a Betty Crocker cookbook. They ate until full. 'Mama' appeared in the dining area from the kitchen to assess the satisfaction of the patrons. Arriving at their table, she asked, "How is everything?"

"Just wonderful," they answered. It truly was.

The name badge proclaimed her to be 'Mama Phipps.' An amazon of a woman, 'Mama' was not about to be slapped by *any*one, at *any* time, for *any* reason, no matter how good *any-*

thing was, on *any* given day, at all! She had a warm glow and charm about her, but one could tell that wrapped inside all her warmth and charm was a force to be reckoned with and dare anyone try. She eyed their plates for any remnants of lingering food.

"Somethin' wrong with that last portion, Suga'?" she asked Jace, while aiming her index finger down toward his plate to an orphaned shrimp, without any accompanying grits.

"No Mam!" he said, and quickly gulped down the last bite. Satisfied, she patted him on the head and parted her way to the next table of unsuspecting victims. They got the impression that no one dared leave any remnants of food on their plate in Mama Phipps' house or suffer her wrath. They tipped Katina handsomely and made their way to the exit. Seeing them leaving, 'Mama' waved and yelled from across the room, "YA'LL COME BACK NOW!" They would.

From the outside, the Wind Drift Bay Apartment Homes were appealing and beautifully landscaped. A sign declared: *Your search is over…Welcome home!* Perry hoped so. It was their first stop. They did a drive around of the complex before circling back to the main entrance and took a FUTURE RESIDENT PARKING spot outside the front office. Inside, a smartly appointed reception area welcomed them. Molly, one of three available leasing agents, was a delight and eager to assist. It did not bode well for Perry that Jace took a particular liking to her.

She took their names and drivers licenses and asked if they were interested in seeing the model. They were. She led them from the office to the apartment unit, where they passed a resort-style swimming pool, complete with a spewing fountain and crystal-clear water to the bottom. There was a canopied picnic area and a shaded jogging trail that led into an adjoining park. It would make for many pleasant evening walks. Covered parking was also a plus. The third-floor apartment was stunning. The front door opened to an expansive living area. To its left was a sunroom with balcony overlooking Lake Royalton. It came to Perry's attention that it was a two-bedroom and two-bath model, with the bedrooms on opposite sides of the apartment facing the lake. They had failed to tell her for *one*. She assumed they were roommates. There was a fully functional kitchen, complete with a pass-through bar and abundant dining space. Other amenities included a washer and dryer, security system, fireplace, and lots of windows. Jace emerged from down a hall, having the same revelation as Perry, *two bedrooms*. Seeing their obvious attraction to the apartment, Molly informed them that it was the last and actual unit available in two bedrooms. All the others were leased.

"Will this do?" she asked them.

"How much?"

"With the special, nine hundred dollars a month," she answered.

Their eyes aglow, Jace and Perry looked at each other for what seemed like an eternity. They desperately wanted to know what the other thought; then finally, with huge smiles on their faces, and as if suddenly having the gift of mind reading, they proclaimed in perfect harmony and unison, "We'll take it!"

"Great!" Molly exclaimed. She led them back to the office to complete the paperwork. They signed a year lease. Leaving the property, they were excited about their new apartment home.

"I hope you're not a slob," Jace said laughingly.

"I hope you're not a neat nick," Perry retorted.

"I don't even know you."

"You soon will."

"Can you cook?" Jace asked.

"Quite well," Perry confirmed.

"Not like my mama," Jace challenged.

"I wouldn't be so sure," Perry countered, knowing well he was probably right.

"One or two phone lines?"

"One. You take the electric bill. I'll pay the phone."

"Will the weasel be joining us?" Perry asked.

"'Fraid so," Jace answered. "And it's called a FERRET!"

"Sure," Perry said, dismissing the correction, "And the boa?"

"Yep," Jace confirmed.

Perry threatened the fearless predator of snakes, a mongoose, if the boa became sassy. That sent Jace doubled over with laughter. It was contagious. They would move-in in thirty days.

They arrived back at Perry's apartment sooner than expected—much sooner. He had anticipated a full day of apartment searching, never expecting to settle on the first property they visited. They both agreed it was an excellent choice, with just the right amenities and extras. Everything seemed to fall into place for them that morning. 'Mama' had filled their stomachs with great food, and blessed them with spiritually uplifting songs in her restaurant. They had found a most incredible place to live, and at a decent price; and by chance, they would now be roommates. Their new living arrangement would be to the delight of Jace's family once they learned of the development. Oh happy day!

CHAPTER FIVE

An Ominous Silence

The night was wet with rain.

Screeching tires were heard in the distance.

Horns sounded their caution.

Sirens echoed the air with cries for help.

A helicopter could be heard overhead.

Hurried footsteps splattered the wet pavement below, as pedestrians sought shelter from the deluge.

A thunderous roar made its presence known.

Lightning lit up the dark and dreary night, if only but for a split second.

The wind howled its fury.

An ominous silence filled the parking garage, interrupted by a reverberating drip of water, its source unknown. The forecasters' predictions of thunderstorms could not have been more accurate. It was a late September evening. Mr. Coffey was in a hurry to get home.

Another threat had arrived at his office and was the most troubling one of all. It came in the form of a video, his wedding day, thirty years ago. He played the tape of the happy occasion on his office TV and VCR combo, wondering how anyone, save family, could have acquired it. Watching, he couldn't help but chuckle to himself at seeing the dated clothing and bouffant hairstyles. The tape showed a lovely Trudy Louise Burgess, adorned in a white chiffon gown, gracing a rose petaled path, as she made her way to the flowered canopy to join her soon-to-be husband. Upon hearing the words, 'You may kiss the bride,' declared by the clergyman, Mr. Coffey raised the veil to a skeletal face of his new wife, hair swooping over her bony head and cheeks, as the piercing and hollow eye chasms' haunting and sustained death stare stared back at him. He kept watching. The video became grainy and flashed on to a hospital delivery room. The skeleton woman lay writhing in pain on the table, finally giving birth to a lifeless baby boy, her first. Stillborn. Mr. Coffey wiped his brow and loosened the tie from around his neck. He wondered how it was possible. The tape rolled on. He recognized the next frame as the baby's room of their first home. The skeleton woman emitted a harrowing wail of sorrow. Her twins, conjoined in the image, had succumbed to Sudden Infant Death Syndrome, SIDS, as it is known. She collapsed to a pile of bones. The death rattle sent a chill down his spine. He stared, paralyzed by the images on the screen. He was fearless in the face of cowardly acts of aggression, but this had cut to the very core of his being: his wife and children. He suspected the perpetrators of the orchestrated threat. It wreaked of of Titan/Hutt, had their signature all over it, he determined. Only they had the means capable of employing such an elaborate production. But how had they gained access to some of his family's most precious and private moments, he wondered. He would reconsider the police and guard protection, and no longer keep the late-night working hours. The video became static then cut to a menagerie of random clips showing everyday people – strangers – in their hurried lives routines at crosswalks, markets, bus stops, traffic snarls, and evening news anchors reporting on the volatile stock market. It ended abruptly with a flag-draped coffin being lowered into the ground before it flashed off. He had served his country well. Visibly shaken, he longed to see his wife and children.

He looked down into the dimly lit stairwell at the daunting descent that awaited him. It was dank and cool.

He remembered leaving his blazer in the car but was in no state to go back and retrieve it. Still shaken over the disturbing video, his downward spiral began. At the ninth landing, the dark silhouette figure of a cat stood huddled in a corner. Arching its back with hairs standing on end, and hissing, signaled the warning for him to keep his distance. He approached cautiously. Arriving at the seventh landing, he found himself a little winded and began to wheeze. He was not in the greatest shape of his life, and had been warned by his physician of the excess weight, stress, and blood pressure. He trekked further downward. Stopping at landing six, he made a fifth attempt at the cell phone. The obnoxious screech of a fax modem echoed in his ear. He continued on. Rounding the stairs to landing five, he caught a glimpse of two objects that sent his heart racing. He picked up the tweed blazer and paisley tie—*his*. Intact, he left them. He jerked himself around for evidence of another being in the stairwell—no one. Slit eyes peered at him through the railings.

The cat was stalking. It leapt and disappeared into the darkness. He called out a nervous 'hello,' only to have his own voice return to answer him with the same. Anxiety set in as he recalled the dancing shadows on the walls. His forehead beaded with perspiration that dripped down his face and seeped into his eyes.

His breathing became heavy and labored. His heart, now racing and pounding fiercely, threatened cardiac arrest. A nauseous feeling arose from his stomach and lingered at the back of his throat. His hands became clammy and cold. In frantic leaps, he arrived at the third landing. There, lay the cat, gutted; its neck had been snapped, a silent kill. He shone a light from his keychain on the carcass. *Maylay*, he thought to himself. *Was it Maylay?* Trembling uncontrollably, he became lightheaded and went into a dizzying spin.

His evening meal spewed from his mouth and down his shirt. He began to choke. A distant ringing was heard over his violent coughing. He reached into his pocket for the cell phone. Relieved and breathless, he said a panicked, "Hello?" The pleasant and soothing voice on the other end was back: *We're sorry, all circuits are busy now; will you please hang up and try your call again.* Again, he did. The recording returned in a muddle of rambled greetings: *Your call cannot be completed…The number you have…As dialed…Is no longer in service…Hang up…Please check the number…Has been disconnected…Try again…All circuits are busy…We're sorry…*

He turned the phone off and back on again only to hear the robotic voice of the operator once more: *Will you please hang…*

Believing it was all just a bad dream, he wondered how much longer until his waking hour. *This can't be happening; it's all just a bad dream*, he kept telling himself, unconvinced of his own reassuring.

"*Somebody shake me, wake me*," he spoke in a desperate plea that filled the void of the stairwell but went unheard by anyone. "*Please!*" He pressed "0" again for the operator. The annoying chirp of a low battery signal now sounded from the cell phone. He began to despair as one ill-fated event was followed by another. His eyes squinting from the burning sweat, he could barely see. In a blinding frenzy, he arrived at the second landing and sat to clear his vision. Opening his eyes, he saw his paisley tie stretched taut at his neck. *Was there no end to his misery*, he thought. *Did God in Heaven have no mercy?* There was no escaping this nightmare; he was already awake, with no time to react in a defensive mode to spare his life.

A quick jerk and he was gasping for air. His legs slowly stopped kicking as the noose tightened, unrelenting in its suffocating hold. His arms suspended their struggling and dropped to his sides. "*I love you, honey*," sputtered from his lips.

An occasional gasp emanated from his lungs. The necktie suddenly loosened and lay draped about his neck. With the last of his strength, he pressed the numbers 9-1-1 on the cell phone. A purposeful voice answered, "This is nine-one-one, what is your emergency?" There was no response.

CHAPTER SIX

The Second Landing

Willie D. Case was a middle-aged man looking to supplement his income. A mechanic by trade and a lanky father of two, it seemed unlikely a part-time job in security of any kind would be fitting for him.

The holstered revolver hanging at his hip offered some comfort and reassurance, and compensated for his emaciated-looking frame. It was a no-brainer job, lacking in excitement, boring, and repetitive. An occasional lockout or jump-start was the most exhilaration he had experienced since taking the part time work for the private security firm in early September that year. It was an opportunity for him to earn extra cash for the rapidly approaching holiday season. His graveyard shift that Friday evening would bring an end to the monotony of his routine.

Most of the employees who worked in the office building—home to the law firm of *Easel, Coffey & Dohme*—had left for the day, Mr. Coffey being one of the last to exit the building. Willie D. had a fondness for the attorney, even considered him a friend, though their friendship did not extend beyond the confined quarters of his employment here. Theirs was like two ships passing in the night, with Willie starting his shift, and Mr. Coffey ending his day. Willie looked forward to their evening chitchats over the current events of the week, and the various happenings in their families' lives. He exited the main building on the tenth floor and crossed through a breezeway that led into the parking tower. Once inside the garage, he made his way to the golf cart that had its reserved spot next to the stairwell. Cranking the ignition and flipping a switch to activate the flashing blue beacon on top, he reversed the gear and then advanced forward to begin his hourly rounds of the parking levels. In the stairwell at landing two, Mr. Coffey lay clinging to life, hoping for any form of medical intervention or first aid that would bring a delay of his progression to death. He had little comfort in the hourly security rounds. The guards seldom went into the stairwells.

Willie had bounced his way down to level five in the golf cart without incident. Stopping here briefly, he got out of the cart to investigate a lone car parked in a handicapped spot without a permissible placard. He noticed nothing else unusual or out of the ordinary and continued on to the remaining levels. Back in the stairwell, Mr. Coffey could hear the motor and feel the vibration of the golf cart as it bounced its way down. Willie descended from the third level. He arrived at the second level and brought the golf cart to a sudden stop. He clearly remembered waving the attorney goodbye up on level ten at the eleven-o'clock hour. But here, parked haphazardly, and in reserved spacing at level two, was the attorney's car. The doors were locked. The attorney's tweed blazer lay across the front seat. His briefcase sat on the passenger floorboard. *He really shouldn't leave it sitting out in the open like that*, Willie thought. *Had he forgotten something and gone back inside?* Reentry into the building after hours would require security access. Willie had not been summoned with a request. It wasn't so unusual, the attorney would routinely meet one of the partners and go out for a cup of coffee, Willie remembered. It seemed a reasonable explanation this time. He continued on to the ground level.

He arrived at the first level and parked the golf cart in its assigned space as before and above, next to the stairwell. It proved another uneventful check of the parking garage. A faint chirping, indicative of a low battery signal from a cell phone or some other electronic device, captured his ear. He got out of the golf cart, immersed in the solitude of the parking garage, and stepped into the stairwell at level one where the chirping became more prominent. At the first landing, he cocked his head and looked up through the spiraling, symmetrical levels of the parking garage stairwell. The chirping echoed clear and audibly from his vantage point. Blood dripped from the third level and splattered the railings below, striking his forehead. The stench of vomit permeated the confined air. A foot dangled at the second landing, seizing him with sudden fear. He removed the revolver from its holster and yelled out, "Hello? Anybody there?" In his last fleeting moments, Mr. Coffey opened his mouth and cried a silent scream. Willie began to ascend the stairwell to investigate the source of the dying battery, and the dangling extremity, and the dripping blood. He took one cautious step at a time, jerking himself around to check for the presence of another being in the stairwell—no one. He arrived at the second landing and held his breath from the offensive odor. In an instant, his heart began to race at what he saw before him. The ghastly figure of a man, tinged a bluish-purple color about his face and neck, and soiled with vomit, lay slumped against the railing with a tie hanging loosely from his neck. "Sir?" he called to the man but got no response. With his arm extended and the revolver aimed, Willie quickly wound his way up to level three to rout out the source of the blood.

There, lay a cat, gutted; its neck had been snapped. He returned to the grisly figure at the second landing and lifted the chin of the man to reveal his identity. He instantaneously fell back against the cinder block concrete wall upon recognition of his friend, the attorney. He had been left there for dead and was dying.

Willie panicked. His hands trembled as he punched the numbers 9-1-1 on his mobile phone. If the attorney stood any chance of survival, it now rested with William D. Case. The monotony of his routine had been broken.

Willie's small frame was no match for the robust build of Mr. Coffey. It took all his might to get him into the supine position and begin CPR. He gave the fifteen chest compressions and two breaths as directed by the 9-1-1 operator, hoping at any moment the attorney would give response to his lifesaving efforts. He received none. The wailing cry of an ambulance could be heard in the distance. An emergency medical services team was soon to arrive. Willie feared it was too late.

CHAPTER SEVEN

Little Boy Lost

Paramedics raced to the garage tower. They arrived to find Mr. Coffey in full cardiac arrest and began their resuscitative protocol. An EKG showed his heart to be in ventricular fibrillation, erratic and non-perfusing, and always fatal if not quickly converted. The paramedics administered a two-hundred-watt shock of electricity in an attempt at jump starting his heart; another at three hundred, still another at three hundred and sixty. A surgical incision was made to his throat with a tube placed inside to access his trachea and provide ventilation. With the first round of emergency drugs on-board, they rushed him to Falls Mercy Hospital.

He was comatose for a week and had suffered some degree of brain damage. Because of the quick response from Willie and the paramedics, it was believed to be mild. Trudy, forever by his side, kept a daily vigil.

Jace and Perry made a visit on day seven, intent on giving her a break from her nightly hospital stays. She refused to leave her husband's side and held out hope for his full recovery as the Thanksgiving and Christmas holidays were rapidly approaching. Sitting around his bed in idle conversation, the trio suddenly noticed a stirring of his legs, a fluttering of his eyes, a rousing of his being. They watched as lions stalking prey.

"Get the doctor!" Trudy insisted, checking his ear for the hearing aid. It was *on*. "Donerson?" she called, but got no response. Dr. Silas Norcroft, a neurologist, and a host of medical personnel entered the room and watched in anticipation. The suspense was unnerving. Placing a hand on the attorney's forehead, Doctor Norcroft leaned over and whispered, "Eugene? Eugene!" His eyes, opening fully now, were fixed on a shelf at the foot of his bed. There, an arrangement of colorful carnations placed in a flowerpot of a hollow wooden boxcar sat, get well soon wishes sent by Hammonds, a local collectibles boutique. Trudy retrieved the flowers and brought them to his bedside, his eyes never leaving the arrangement. She sat them just below his chest. With a slow arm moving forward, his fingers began to gently feel along the top of the boxcar flowerpot.

"Eugene?" Norcroft whispered again, and again there was no response.

It was another three days before he spoke. The flower arrangement, wilted now, remained the source of his attention. He'd spend hours caressing the boxcar. Trudy's attempt at removing the dried carnations was met with instant and grunting opposition from him. Startled by this, she called out to him, "Eugene?"

"What mommy? I didn't do it, don't take my train," came the voice of a child from her husband.

Trembling, she pressed the nurse 'call' button at his bedside remote.

"Can I help you?" a female's voice asked through the intercom. Mrs. Coffey, her mouth agape, was speechless. Dr. Norcroft had warned her of the possibility of him reverting to his childhood. She had not prepared herself for this. A petite, certified nurse aide entered the room. Seeing Mrs. Coffey visibly shaken, she called out to the patient, "Mr. Coffey?" He did not answer. "Eugene?" she called.

"I've been a baaad boy I have, and mommy wants to take my train. Tell her I'll be good. Honest, I will, honest engine," the 'child' replied, while raising his right hand in affirmation of the truth. "Scout's honor," he continued, now holding his pinky finger down with his thumb. The aide summoned Dr. Norcroft.

"Mommy, my wee-wee go pee-pee…mommy?" the 'boy' continued, as the output level of his urinary catheter bag increased. Hearing no response from his 'mommy,' the 'little boy,' now panicked, let out a frantic, shrill cry as if lost in a crowded amusement park, "MOMMEEE!" The aide tried calming the 'child,' but to no avail. "I WANT MY MOMMY!" he insisted, yelling at her. *His* mother had died years ago. The man-child, now arising from the bed, began to visually scan the room in search of 'his' mother. His eyes locked onto Trudy. "What have you done with my mommy?" He snapped angrily before hurling a glass at her, it shattering upon impact with the wall. His wife, wild-eyed and struggling to ward off an impending faint, offered no response to his pleas. The nurse aide tried to subdue the now combative man-boy as he attempted to climb out of the bed. With a swift and powerful blow to her head, and using all of his might, he pushed her off, sending her sailing across the room and slamming into a wall. Mrs. Coffey went unconscious.

The hospital's security arrived to find a flurry of activity inside. The room was in complete disarray.

Flowers were strewn about. Linens lay hanging in various places. The rolling tray table had been overturned with the evening meal. The nurse aide, slumped in a corner and frothing at the mouth, was in a violent seizure. Her head thumped rhythmically and repeatedly against the blood-stained concrete wall; only the 'whites' of her eyes were visible. An unconscious Mrs. Coffey lay stiff in a pool of spilt liquids.

The 'little boy' was missing.

CHAPTER EIGHT

Death, Defied

He was found sipping hot tea with an elderly patient in the hospital's atrium courtyard, unaware of the trauma he had inflicted in his alter ego state. Security, with Norcroft and a medic, escorted him to another room, urine bag in tow. Although the rooms were identical, he quickly became aware they were not the same. Perplexed, he began to assess the new surroundings. There, on the same shelving as before, was the boxcar. He relaxed. Mrs. Coffey regained consciousness and went into hysterics. Bordering on delirium, she was prescribed a sedative and ordered home for bed rest. The nurse aide was hurried to the Emergency Room, then Intensive Care Unit. She was not expected to live.

Mr. Coffey entered the rehabilitation unit of Falls Mercy Hospital fourteen days after the garage attack. He had spent the latter part of September and most of October that year in the hospital. Sitting in bed feeding himself, he had no recollection of the event that had put him there. Many days would catch him staring out the window at nothing, just staring. The dead carnations were long gone, only the boxcar remained, and still enamored him. Trudy, seeing his delight in the inanimate object, brought more of the same. Soon his room was filled with train cars of different shapes, sizes, colors, and some with spinning wheels even. He was ecstatic.

"Golly-jee willikers, mommy, tank you berry much," her 'little boy' husband said. He would soon graduate to model trains—electric ones. His speech interspersed between child and adolescent babble, and adult coherency.

His mind would forever guard the secret of that late Friday evening. Tomorrow he would start physical therapy, and if all went according to plan, he'd be reintroduced to driving. Doctor Norcroft proclaimed it to be a remarkable transition.

Willie D. Case would call in for his graveyard security shift at the office building where he moonlighted.

He had received an urgent phone call from the hospital. Something terrible had happened. He was given very few details over the telephone but was told to get there as quickly as possible. He immediately suspected that his friend, the attorney, had taken a turn for the worst. The hospital's administrator met him, accompanied by two ICU physicians. They led him to the unit. His wife, a certified nurse aide, lay in one of the beds, comatose, and on a ventilator. The two doctors caught him as his legs gave way. They sat him down.

"I don't understand," he cried. "Wha-what happened? How did…? Why?" He was told the circumstances surrounding his wife's condition. The administrator offered an apology and gave assurances that she would receive the highest quality of care. Willie sat there painfully processing what he had just been told, while dabbing an occasional drip from his nose. After a self-imposed moment of quiet contemplation, his blood-shot eyes widened and became incensed with rage and perfect hatred. "I'll kill him!" he vowed in revenge.

Doctor Norcroft continued to be amazed at Mr. Coffey's remarkable progress. There was talk of his eventual discharge. Trudy delighted in knowing he would be home for the approaching holiday season.

Jace and Perry had made another visit from Royalton and arrived at the hospital's physical therapy unit to see him walking down the hall with the therapist.

"Hello, dad," Jace spoke.

"Mornin', son," he acknowledged.

"Where's mom?"

"In the cafeteria getting coffee. Take her home. She fusses over me like a mother hen over her brood. It's a bit much, son."

"She's only concerned, dad," Jace affirmed.

"I'm not so sure," his father replied.

"Well of course she is, pop," Jace asserted.

"Son, your mother says I have penile dementia." Jace chuckled at his father's error of words.

"It's *senile* dementia, dad," he corrected. "She was being facetious. You simply don't remember like you used to."

"…And that I'm mentally anorexic," his father continued.

"Your minds not as sharp as it used to be *only* because of the accident," Jace reassured.

"What accident? Has there been an accident? Was anybody hurt? Is everybody okay?"

"Never mind," Jace answered.

"What about my demented penis?" his father asked.

"Your penis is not demented," Jace declared.

"Anorexic?"

"That neither."

"How would you know?"

"I don't."

"Is that why I'm here?"

"No."

"Why then?" his father asked. Jace, stumbling for an answer, nudged Perry for assistance. Perry shrugged his shoulders in a gesture of, I don't know.

Mr. Coffey rambled on, "This is really quite confusing. I mean…my pecker…demented or anorexic? Or both! *A screwy, starved schlong,"* he thought to himself, then announced aloud in a raised voice. Jace shushed him.

His father continued, "…Go to bed happy with your pickle and plums, and wake up the next morning with a lunatic dick. This is all your mother's fault. If I've told her once, I've told her a thousand times, 'Love the dick. The dick is your friend. Consider it. Confide in it. Honor it.'

Why, she's way too rough with it, riding it like a bronco. 'It's not a toy, *Louise*…some…plaything.' This is what separates the men from the boys," he continued, proudly reaching down his pants for the obvious. The therapist stops him.

"Keep your voice down," Jace whispered, suddenly aghast and uncomfortable with the direction their dialogue had taken, and looking around for anyone in earshot of the conversation.

"Mother meant no harm in saying that," he said to reassure his father and end the discussion.

"Saying what, son?" his father further questioned. Jace, completely flustered, stammered and stuttered for words, then finally blurted out, "Defective," instead of his intended demented.

"DEFECTIVE!" His father denounced, becoming increasingly agitated, before going off on a tangent: "My dick is NOT defective. Car parts are 'defective.' They break, you send them back to the dealership to be repaired or replaced, right? How dare you denigrate my dick to that of a dipstick when I blasted you from it. Remember your origins. Satisfaction guaranteed, *or what?* My money back? And if she's not 'completely satisfied?' *Who* do I send *it* back to? Mother won't like this. She won't like this one bit."

"Your mother is dead, dad," Jace said, completely exasperated and giving in to defeat.

"OH YEAH!" his father's alter ego snapped, "…Well *YO* mama so *FAT*, she makes Tyrannosaurus Rex look like a gecko!"

"Dad!" Jace rebuked.

"Your pap ain't here, ya little twerp. Besides, my dad can lick your dad's ass ANY day!" 'Junior' challenged. "Were you born stupid or was it something you picked up along the way?" he continued. Mr. Coffey, in his child-like persona, scowled at Perry, looked him up and down and declared, "I see you picked it up along the way. Stupid…Anorexic…Dick…Dumb…Penis…Ass," he insulted, taunting his son. The therapist intervened, motioning him toward his room.

"Ah yes, thank you, Dear" Mr. Coffey said calmly. "Do try and get her home, son. She needs the rest."

Not knowing if he still possessed the ability to operate a car, Dr. Norcroft, with the therapist, decided to test the waters in a remote corner of the hospital parking lot. An obstacle course had been set up with some tricky maneuvering. He mastered it beautifully, knocking over only one cone. To their surprise, he retook to driving unscathed. He had regained all of his motor skills in therapy: walking, running, exercise, hand-eye coordination, even tying a tie. Physically, he had made a one-hundred-dred-percent recovery.

His mental state improved as well with only occasional outbursts from 'Junior.' He could carry on simple conversation, but any topics of higher reasoning were frustrating. They were avoided. Doctor Norcroft suggested this would be the Eugene

Coffey of today, and quite possibly, the rest of his life. He would likely not work as an attorney again, a job far too complex for him now. At the downtown law offices of *Easel, Coffey & Dohme*, he was given early retirement with a handsome severance package. He was released from Falls Mercy Hospital on Monday, thirty-two days after the garage attack. It was late October. Attorney Donerson Eugene Coffey had battled Death. And won.

CHAPTER NINE

Act One, Scene Two

Back at the Christmas gathering, Trudy had put the finishing touches on her famous dressing and summoned the family to the dining table. Dinner, as expected, was excellent but not without fanfare. It turned out to be a stage drama with Mr. Coffey in the lead role. Threatening to boycott the feast because of his earlier chastening from Trudy over his 'bovine' remark of Jessyca, he conceded and assumed his position at the head of the table. He would do the honor of saying grace. Mr. Coffey was notorious for his table blessings that would oftentimes evolve into a sermonette and bear no relevance to the giving of thanks or the meal at hand. Without fail, an excerpt of locomotive history would somehow bore its way into his 'thanks' giving, as he felt a need to pay homage to the era during this sacred time. The Christmas dinner grace was to be the pinnacle of his table blessings. Scripted. Rehearsed. Practiced. He'd spent a month in preparation for this very moment. The 'stage' would be his and the one time he would command the spotlight. It was his moment to shine. He took full advantage of the opportunity, reveling in the attention and basking in his own glory. Any interruption by his audience would be cause for immediate expulsion from the table and eventual starvation as he saw it. At stake was the famed and winning dressing. Trudy, invariably, would tire of his table tomfoolery and bring an end to his mealtime shenanigans, the Christmas dinner blessing being her one exception. And so, like a captive audience, they waited for him to recite the grace.

"Bow your heads," he boomed, like a preacher ready to deliver a fervent prayer. Simultaneously, they bowed their heads. A defiant Trudy chose to remain alert for what she suspected to be another one of his monologue blessings and did not drop her head. Subsequently, a skirmish ensued with Mr. Coffey because of her, as he put it, "rebellion." He accused his wife of sabotaging his much practiced and rehearsed soliloquy. Entering stage left, Maylay strutted in to investigate the interruption source of her noon nap, and to make her disapproval known; she then took her place underneath the table. The cat had used up eight of her 'nine lives' where Mr. Coffey was concerned, and the ninth one hung in the balance at that very moment. He detested the rubbing up against his leg by the feline, believing it was a signal to the others to exact revenge on him. Convinced that Trudy and Maylay had plotted against him backstage, and that mutiny was on the brink, he bolted from his chair, wielding the carving knife, one foot on the table, the other in the seat of his chair. Fearing amputation of some body part, Jace and the others dove for safety underneath the table. Maylay, her domain intruded upon, decided she had more important business in another part of the house, abandoned the sudden assembly and sauntered off casually. Stopping at the door, she turned and gave a disapproving hiss to Mr. Coffey, before making her exit. Trudy, unruffled by her husband's antics, remained at the table.

"Friends! Romans! Countrymen! Lend me your ears," he belted. Trudy simply stared at him, as she had so many times before, her facial expression showing painful realization at a once brilliant mind lost forever.

Reluctantly, she let him continue. Jace and the others gradually emerged from below and reclaimed their places at the table. With the knife 'at ease,' Mr. Coffey looked around in embarrassment, and with the countenance of one who had just made an audible passage of gas, with the odor soon to follow. *He had.*

The excitement proved too much for him. He slowly took his seat and looked at Trudy in bewilderment.

"It's okay, honey," came the reassurance from his wife as she patted his hand.

"What in the hell was it?" He mumbled in confusion.

"Just a little disruption by the Romans," she chuckled.

"Damn Romans!" he added. Squirming in his seat, he uttered sheepishly, "I, uhm, seem to have soiled myself."

"It would appear," Jace said, contorting his face from the stench.

"Indeed!" Alex confirmed. Jessyca began a slow oscillation of her hand to fan away the offending fumes.

Kali, attempting to remain dignified and poised, spat up something of an ill consistency. Jessyca reveled in her display of *dis*grace. Perry had made it up to count fifty-two in the holding of his breath and desperately needed air. Alex and Asher made a hasty departure while the odor dissipated. "Dammit, Don!" Trudy inadvertently let slip, before coming to her husband's rescue and ushering him away to the bathroom. 'Intermission' over, she returned him afresh. The smell, now in the confines of the atmosphere, was gone. The twins made a triumphant return. Kali, still reeling over her public display of spit-up, tried to regain her composure and return herself to a state of elegance and grace. Jessyca gave a vivid account of the 'upchuck,' describing in great detail, and with demonstration, Kali's facial expression, mouth positioning and head swagger as the mess came slopping out. She offered snide amazement at how one so beautiful could expel something so foul, finally comparing it to the rancid release by Mr. Coffey. Kali was mortified and on the verge of collapse. Jessyca fanned her with a limp napkin in a gesture of concern. Trudy spouted off the shortest bible verse, 'Jesus wept,' as a form of grace and began passing around their plates. Mr. Coffey expertly carved the turkey and divvied out the portions. With the 'show' now over, they enjoyed the meal. Soon after, Mr. Coffey interrupted the various table conversations with the clinking of a fork against his glass to seize their attention. He had what he deemed to be an important announcement. He removed the cloth napkin tucked in his collar and dabbed each corner of his mouth, piquing their curiosity. Commanding their full attention was his mentioning of a special, "limited-edition" boxcar at Hammonds, the local collectibles boutique. It would add to his already extensive train collection but was of no immediate interest to those gathered at the table. He had reserved his well in advance. It would be a few more weeks before the joyous day of its arrival at Hammonds. He anticipated it like a child would his birthday. Trudy and the others displayed animated expressions at the meaningless bulletin before resuming their conversations and eating.

"Big outfit like that oughta be more expeditious," he blurted out, as an afterthought. Hammonds Collectibles was a small mom and pop shop in town, run by a retired couple on a fixed income. They all halted their feeding and pondered his "expeditious," wondering from what remote corner of his altered state he had pulled it from. He never ceased to amaze.

After dinner the family gathered in the living room around the haphazardly dressed Douglas fir for the exchange and opening of gifts. Mr. Coffey had helped in the decorating of the tree and made his hodge-podge appointments known. Most notably, was his placement of a sizable – and flashing – railroad crossing X atop the tree, instead of the traditional star or angelic being. Dinging bells, identical to those signaling the immediate downing of railroad crossing arms to block vehicle passage and alert drivers and pedestrians to an approaching train, sounded every thirty seconds throughout the house. Trudy humored him by praising the addition, fearing another one of his outbursts otherwise. And in his Christmas day songs rotation on the stereo, he had, *I've Been Working on the Railroad, Midnight Train to Georgia,* and Quad City DJs' *C'mon 'N' Ride It (The Train),* in that order, and on repeat. And when the chorus line of, "Dinah, won't you blow your horn," came 'round, he did exactly that, from a kazoo tucked inconspicuously in his coveralls front pocket, each time. Trudy was spent.

Alex and Asher made their way to the den where football could be heard on the television. They had a wager on the game. Football was the one thing that competed with the trains to create a temporary diversion of Mr. Coffey. Ultimately, the trains would prevail as his interest in the sport waned. The game, in the second quarter with the opposing team losing, was enough to send him scurrying off to his locomotive world. Back in the living room, Perry sat in an oversized and over-stuffed leather chair, savoring a slice of the pumpkin pie with a dollop of whipped topping. Trudy and Jessyca were huddled over a photo album. Kali sat alone, busily logging an entry into her journal and reflecting on the dinner table debacle and her humiliating contribution to it. She had been unusually dis-tant since arriving. Asher confessed that they were having rela-tionship struggles but assured the family of nothing serious. Wedding bells were in their future.

Mr. Coffey had retreated to the foyer from the living room where he could be heard angrily scolding someone over God-only-knows-what. There had not been a knock on the door or a ring of the bell to rescue an unsuspecting visitor from his vitriolic attack. Jace went to investigate the source of his father's raging. The recipient of his disgruntlement was Maylay. The cat was perched on the window ledge, in usual fashion, minding her own business, and with her back turned to Mr.

Coffey, as he continued launching verbal assaults at her. There had been another derailment of the train set and Maylay just so happened to be at the 'crime' scene at an inopportune time, assuring her immediate guilt by Mr. Coffey. Jace calmed his father, retrieved the displaced train cars, and got things back on track. He and Perry would make the trip back to Royalton tomorrow, the twins back to Common Wells. Trudy began gathering their plates and started tidying up from dinner, refusing all offers of help. Alex and Asher left to visit friends, taking Jessyca and Kali with them. Mr. Coffey kept himself amused with the trains. Jace joined Perry in the living room and stretched out comfortably on the matching sleeper sofa. He lay resting peacefully, as peaceful as a newborn baby. Perry watched him.

CHAPTER TEN

Wine and Water

Jace and Perry left Provident Falls the following day. Trudy saw them off with her usual care package of goodies and treats. A substantial portion of her prized dressing was also included. Jace was anxious to get back to Royalton, having had his fill of the family, but also with anticipation of his date with Molly on Sunday. Perry was withdrawn and in a somber mood as he reflected on the thirty-first anniversary of his mother's death. They took the interstate freeway back. It was a boring drive but considerably faster than the more scenic US highway system that brought them over. Jace was behind the wheel and shared one of his father's characteristics, a 'lead' foot. They now found themselves sitting idle on the shoulder of the freeway with red and blue beacons flashing around them. Earlier in the drive, Perry had warned Jace of his near-ninety miles per hour acceleration as they raced past the other freeway travelers at blistering speeds.

Through some stroke of luck or divine intervention, the state trooper released them after issuing Jace a warning citation, saving him from a costly fine. Jace gladly accepted the officer's reprimand and relaxed his foot for the remainder of the drive.

Christmas had come and gone. Jace and Perry spent a quiet New Year's Eve at home alone. They watched Dick Clark from Times Square and toasted in the New Year with sparkling cider at the midnight hour to the singing of *Auld Lang Syne*. Soon after, Jace went to bed with thoughts of his New Year's date with Molly.

She was the same Molly who had shown them their apartment some five months earlier. Since that time, she and Jace had exchanged text messages and phone calls with promises of getting together that never materialized. His date with her on Sunday was nothing of what he had anticipated it to be. Ironically, she, too, was a married woman, though separated, whose husband, she complained, was not *there* for her. Her words rang familiar as he had been accused of the very same. Jace suddenly found himself in the position of being the 'other' man. He wanted no part of the triangle and quickly abandoned the thought of seeing her again.

It was early on when he inquired about Perry's significant female other. Perry concocted a story of how *his* imaginary girl conveniently lived in another city far away, their relationship on shaky ground because of the distance he added for believability. He knew he would eventually have to produce a name, picture, or detailed account of some fictitious rendezvous with a female liaison to satisfy Jace's curiosity. Jace introduced the idea of a double date. Perry pretended to embrace the thought. To his bluff, it had already been arranged. His attempts to weasel out of it were futile.

Their names were Chianti and Aqua. *Wine and water*, Perry joked, realizing a kinship between the girls' names and those of female dancers in a Gentleman's Only establishment. Not surprisingly, *they were*. Jace had met them before his move from Sheffield and had taken a special interest in Aqua. Trudy, the religious voice of reason for the family, did not favor the idea of him seeing another woman until his divorce was final, but was cordial to his new female love interest nonetheless during her visits to the home with Jace.

Roommates themselves, Chianti and Aqua were looking forward to the date, Jace eagerly informed.

"Great," Perry cheered, with about as much enthusiasm as an IRS audit notice. They would pick them up at seven. Dinner at eight. Dancing at nine. Live music from Alex's band at eleven. It had all been planned.

Perry practiced a cross-eyed stare, lisp, and uncoordinated gait in hopes of not appealing to either of the girls. What to wear? He debated.

It was late afternoon. Perry had no time for his regular gym visit before the date. Subsequently, he decided to do some bicep curls, push-ups, and abdominal crunches in the sunroom. Jace had a clear view of Perry's workout from the living room where he was watching a National Geographic program on public television.

Perry disrobed to a pair of boxer briefs and socks, catching a shy glance from Jace who was sitting on the sofa. Jace quickly turned away at Perry's observation of being watched by him. Lifting the substantial weight, Perry began to curl the bar upward toward his chest. The veins in his arms engorged as his biceps bulged in response. Dropping to the floor, he did a set of fifty push-ups and crunches. He would repeat these for another two rounds. Perry's last set succeeded in diverting Jace's attention away from the television and a feeding frenzy on the Serengeti plains, to his workout. He now stood leaning against a wall with his hands stuffed in his pockets intently watching Perry. Neither spoke. Perry picked up the curl bar for the last set of reps. His body grunted in protest as he neared the final few. Jace, seeing him struggle with the last two, came forward and placed the fingers of one hand under the bar to assist him in the final 'push.'

Perry winked and smiled at him in a gesture of thanks. Jace nodded and reassumed his position against the wall, his gaze fixed on Perry's physique in admiration. Perry, keenly aware that he was being watched, remembered Asher's words as spoken by Jace, 'Says he's even inspired to work out if his body could look like yours.' He was flattered by the notion. He finished the push-ups, and then lay on his back with knees bent for the final set of crunches. Jace knelt at his ankles and held them as Perry began the seesaw motions, a show of embarrassment on his face because of their near intimate connection.

After completing the set, Perry let out an exhausted, *"Whew!"* Jace disappeared into the kitchen and returned with a bottle of sports drink, handing it to Perry. Perry thanked him and took a swig. Jace returned a boyish grin then grabbed the bottle from Perry, taking a gulp for himself. Inspired by Perry's workout, Jace then walked over to the curl bar and picked it up with strained effort. Perry removed some of the weight plates and stood behind him to show the proper technique, requiring him to wrap his arms around Jace's torso. Jace glanced down and from side to side at the muscled forearms and biceps that now held him. He shuddered in Perry's embrace. Perry then placed a palmed hand inside of Jace's inner thigh to spread his legs shoulders width apart for balance and stance. Jace squirmed at his touch. He completed a total of ten curls. Perry congratulated him and suggested they start getting ready for the date. It was nearing seven o'clock. Jace stared at him. Reluctantly, he agreed. Perry turned and headed for the shower. He removed his briefs as he walked away. Jace's stare continued. Perry wore only the socks now that were gathered at his ankles, giving Jace a glimpse of his profile as he turned and disappeared into the bathroom. Splattering water from the shower followed.

Perry emerged from the bathroom with a towel draped loosely just below his waist. He could hear an increased volume of the television. Back in the living room, Jace had returned to the arid plains of the African Serengeti, having made no effort at readying himself for the date. Perry scolded him for his delay in getting dressed and warned they were likely going to be late. To his confusion, Jace suggested they cancel the date for another time. Perry, no more enthused about the date as Jace suddenly appeared not to be either, considered the idea of not going, then decided it would not be the proper thing to do. The girls were waiting on them. He didn't want to stand them up. He took the remote from Jace, aimed it at the television and pressed the POWER button. The screen blinked off. Jace leaned back on the sofa with his arms extended and his elbows resting on its back. He remembered Perry's promise to tell of an English term paper experience and reminded him of it now.

"So tell me about this English term paper," Jace said, attempting to further delay their planned outing.

"Are you nuts?" Perry asked rhetorically. "This date was *your* idea, remember? We're already late." He pulled Jace up by his arm and instructed him to go and get dressed. Jace resisted. Perry then jokingly asked.

"Do you need help?" Jace looked at Perry standing before him, still draped in the towel and glistening from his shower, and answered, "Yes. Do you?"

"Very funny," Perry answered, dismissing the remark.

"I'm not laughing," Jace replied. *He wasn't.*

CHAPTER ELEVEN

An Evening to Remember

Perry decided on a 1970s look. He wore plaid, retro pants with flared bottoms and a long-sleeved polyester shirt with a prominent collar. Jace opted for black jeans and a turtleneck pullover. They arrived at the girls' apartment fashionably late. When Chianti answered the door, Perry's mouth dropped. An exquisite being, she would bear his children if he were so inclined. She was an inch shorter than Jace and had short cropped brown hair, green eyes, and silky-smooth chocolate skin. Plump lips and ample cleavage completed her perfection. Chianti invited them inside. Jace made the necessary introductions. She offered Perry her hand, with perfectly manicured nails and the softness of a baby's bottom. Her smile was intoxicating. Perry was awestruck. His tongue refused to speak fluidly. They took their seats on the sofa. Aqua presented herself, giving him a double dose of beauty. She had long shapely legs, unencumbered by pantyhose, which complemented an above-the-knee mini skirt at her waist. They engaged in small talk. Jace joked with the girls as though they were long lost friends. Perry excused himself to the bathroom. Upon his return, they headed out and would take his car.

They arrived at the restaurant, turning the heads of a few patrons as they waded through the dining room to their table. Bristol, their waiter, was of Mediterranean descent and was strikingly handsome with perfect teeth and a friendly smile. He arrived with a bottle of house wine to pour their glasses, casting a wistful glance at Perry as he circled the table to fill their goblets. He would return for their orders. The conversation with Chianti and Aqua abolished Perry's preconceived notions of the girls. To their credit, both were students. Dancing was a way of getting them through school. They danced at a club called *Male Call,* and sometimes worked as a team on the platforms. Not surprisingly, their routine was dubbed 'the turning of water into wine.' *Apropos,* given their stage names, Perry concluded. He had only known of One to conquer that feat. Their rendition would undoubtedly prove more provocative, even sacrilegious to some.

Bristol returned with a complimentary basket of bread, accompanied with whipped butter, and placed it in the center of the table. He removed a pen and paper from his apron to take their orders. Starting with the girls, he wrote down their dinner selections and collected their menus before darting off. Ten minutes later, their food arrived in an impressive display of creativity. Bristol refilled their glasses before making his exit.

Their real names were Haley, a/k/a, Chianti, and Karter. Haley was a med student on a full scholarship with ambitions of becoming a thoracic surgeon. Karter would delve into the tech world of computer sciences.

She was footing her education bill alone. Their dancing was paying the tuition for now, though wearing on her as she grew tired of the routine; but having too much month left at the end of her paycheck, and mounting financial obligations and tuition expenses, compelled her to continue. Bristol made his final appearance with the check and handed it to Perry. Tucked inconspicuously inside the receipt wallet was a small slip of paper. A smiley face grinned at him. Bristol's number was below, with a scribbled message instructing Perry to call. Jace would be picking up the tab and held out his hand for the ticket. Perry handed it to him, keeping the slip of paper from Bristol and tucking it inside his pants pocket. They left the restaurant and headed for the dance club.

The repetitive techno beat of *Mussolini's* thumped to the outside. Perry warily handed his ignition key to a teen-aged-looking driver who took the car and sped away. They presented their IDs to a Goliath of a man outside the main entrance. The bouncer dictated those allowed admission based upon their "look." He gave them clearance to enter. A cloud of smoke engulfed them once inside. The dense crowd was made up of people from all walks of life, sexualities, genres, and attitudes. They made their way to the bar. Haley and Perry had already begun to bounce to the rhythmic beat of the music. After a drink, they were ready to move and bumped their way to the dance floor holding hands. Jace and Karter found a table in a dark corner of the club and watched the crowd. The dance floor was alive with partygoers flailing their arms, twisting their bodies, and shuffling their feet to the energizing rumble that vibrated the hardwood floor from the strategically placed speakers. Haley and Perry joined in the frenzy. After an extended play of the techno beat, the music mixed into a slow, erotic groove. With an arm cradling the small of her back, Perry purposely pulled Haley into him and they began a sensual gyrating motion of their hips, drawing the attention of those around them. Their bodies melded together like the pieces of a puzzle. They were oblivious to the stares. Haley decided it necessary to untuck Perry's shirt and undo the buttons, leaving his chest and abs exposed. Perry began to perspire. Haley ran her hands down his chest, firmly gripping his pecs and touching him in places a mother would frown upon. Perry cupped her inviting breasts without hesitation. She moaned in tacit approval. They became the main attraction on the dance floor. Their eyes locked. Perry held her face with the palms of his hands and thrust his tongue deep inside her mouth, tasting the sweet nectar from her soft and succulent lips. Haley grabbed the back of his head and pushed forward to further advance the penetration, her nails burying into his scalp. He felt a surge in his briefs as her nipples swelled and then hardened. She consumed his tongue deep inside her mouth, probing it with hers before release. Her gentle caress continued downward, brushing across the head of his rigidity, and causing a buckling of his knees and certain collapse if one more touch. Perry grabbed the offending hand and returned the favor of his tongue to her fingers. He held her ever closer to him, concealing his protrusion in her high-waisted, pleated skirt until flaccid again. The music segued back to the thunderous roar of the techno beat. Haley and Perry returned to reality and found themselves encircled by the voyeuristic crowd. They laughed their way off the dance floor in search of Jace and Karter, who had watched the entire spectacle from an upstairs balcony. After another round of drinks, they all retreated downstairs for more dancing before leaving the club.

Alex was the lead singer in a local band playing Royalton. Their sound had a soothing affect, allowing them to unwind from *Mussolini's* as they sat with their respective dates. He proudly announced their presence to the intimate crowd and went over to their table and offered drinks. "Four coffees," they insisted. The band began its last set. Jace spotted Jessyca and invited her to join them. She stumbled over, having had a bit much to drink and plopped her mass at their table. Introductions were made. Her drunken cackle was more than they could bear at the late hour. They prepared to go after finishing their coffees.

Alex waved them bye from the stage. It was nearing midnight. Haley and Karter decided a dip in the hot tub would complete the evening.

They arrived back at the ladies' apartment. Jace and Perry had not come prepared for the hot tub. Haley and Karter anticipated this and produced two new pair of swim trunks for them. The two gentlemen excused themselves to make their changes. Jace emerged clad only in the form fitting trunks, with a towel draped over his shoulder. Perry was reminded of his remarkable legs. Haley and Karter had already taken their places in the water. Jace and Perry made necessary adjustments to their trunks and sought coverage from their arousals beneath the bubbling water and spewing jets. As the minutes ticked by, there was a lull in the conversation. They felt themselves growing tired. Jace fought to keep his head up as he nodded with drowsiness. The ladies thanked them for a fun evening, with anticipation of a future one. Karter went to gather their clothes. Jace stood up in the hot tub unsteadily. Perry placed an arm around his waist to support him, as Jace draped his arm around Perry's neck. Perry held it with his other hand. They stumbled to the car and rode home wearing only the swim trunks, catching a witty, goodbye pageant wave from a beaming Karter as they drove off. Jace fell asleep on the front seat. Realization of their near nakedness became apparent once they arrived back at their apartment. Supporting Jace once more, Perry hurried him inside. The feel of their smooth bare skin gave rise to their male vehicles. Ignoring the obvious they parted ways to their bedrooms. They would not soon forget this evening.

PART TWO

CHAPTER TWELVE

There She Is, Miss America

The home offices of Titan/Hutt Industries, Incorporated, were in the gulf coastal city of Houston, Texas, and spanned an entire downtown block of the bustling and crowded metropolis. A conservatively dressed female wearing a navy skirt suit entered the dominant tower of the sprawling office complex. In a city with a population surpassing two million, she could have easily been mistaken for any one of the thousands of employees who reported to work each morning at the office building. She wasn't. Having claimed turf on Houston's infamous Bissonnet Blade, notorious for its "specialty services," she saw opportunity as a means to an end of escaping her clandestine side hustle once and for all. She had long, brunette hair that was not hers, swathed in a scarf, and wore dark pointed sunglasses. The woman took a lobby elevator up to the thirty-second floor of the office tower. Once there, she got off and took a connecting elevator up to the sixty-fourth floor. Access to the top ten floors was restricted. They were occupied by Titan/Hutt. She was met by Landon Hutt, a harried-looking gentleman in his mid-thirties and son of the industry mogul, who took her beyond floor sixty-four, into a world of high stakes, big money, power, and espionage. There was still the matter of Donerson Eugene Coffey to contend with. Despite the attorney's diminished capacity, Titan/Hutt executives still believed him to be a threat to the Hutt powerhouse. A return to his full sanity was not an impossibility, they concluded, and that was a problem for them. They wanted him permanently silenced so as to move on with yet another appeal for construction of their processing plant in Provident Falls. Their threats had not succeeded in thwarting his diligence against them. But Titan/Hutt, whether knowingly or unaware, had been dealt a winning hand. Successes were aligning in their favor. A reprieve had been circumstantially granted unto them through the series of events besieging the attorney. There was consolation in knowing that *candidate* Donerson Coffey would not be vying for a council seat run in the district of the proposed plant, as previously rumored, and that his law practice would be on an indefinite hiatus. A significant blow by way of the garage attack, for which they disavowed knowledge of, had been dealt to him. To further tip the scale in their favor, Titan/Hutt had an ace-in-the-hole. Word of the nurse aide attack at the hospital had reached their offices. Willie D. Case had vowed revenge for the incapacitating of his wife, who still lay comatose in the ICU. He seemed a likely accomplice. Titan/Hutt had the means, and the money, if he had the desire. But under no circumstances would they take refuge in those favorable events. Still, some inside help would be needed. Landon was tasked with spying on the Coffey family and to find a weak link, a "Judas" among them. He watched the goings and comings of the Coffey home on Galatian Avenue from a nearby corner, and saw the woman he would meet on the sixty-fourth floor enter the house. Once she was inside, he crept to her unlocked car parked at the curb. Her purse was tucked inconspicuously underneath the front seat. Securing her drivers license and social security card, he jotted down the necessary information and numbers and left everything just as he had found. Back at their offices, he ran her credit report that wallowed in the lower 500s. Financially, she was in a mess, seemingly living from paycheck to paycheck. At first glance, no one would ever suspect, though her car would blow her sophisticated cover and give clue to her financial woes, precisely the type of person preyed upon by Titan/Hutt for their nefarious undertakings.

She was promised a substantial monetary offering for her assistance. They gave assurances of no illegalities. Her participation would render her debt-free and a comfortable lifestyle upon successful completion of the mission. Her close connection to the Coffey family deemed her the most likely to be successful in their resolve. But the road to financial freedom would require her to betray the very people she loved. Landon had found the weak link. Titan/Hutt had infiltrated the Coffey family by way of *Miss America*.

Landon escorted her down a narrow corridor that led to the office of his father. Above her head, she noticed red blinking lights from security cameras anchored in the ceiling corners. They turned at a hall junction and came to a set of frosted double glass doors. He punched a series of numbers on a wall keypad and swiped a card taken from his coat pocket. A rapid sequence of bleeps sounded.

"Step back," he told her. The heavy doors swung slowly outward as they entered and closed quickly behind them. The offices took on a new dimension, as if they had entered another world. A receptionist announced their arrival via intercom. They were granted clearance to enter. Priceless artwork lined the hardwood mahogany walls. A large window behind the desk gave a spectacular view of Houston's skyline from the seventy-fifth floor. To their immediate right was a wet bar and kitchenette; to their left, a private bath, complete with shower and jetted spa. She was awestruck, having never been exposed to such embellishments. It was the quintessential office setting.

The renowned Maccabeus Hutt was an imposing creature. Arising from his leather-clad wingback chair, he towered over them and was as wide as he was tall. His deep raspy voice made the hairs on her forearms stand on end. He extended a hand to Miss America and offered her a drink. A bottle of designer water was retrieved from the bar for her. Maccabeus dealt strictly with business and had no occasion for idle chatter or meaningless pleasantries. They proceeded with the matter at hand. Being held hostage by her debt, the lure of fast money would compromise her principles. A hefty token of what was to come would be paid immediately, quenching a desire for more. She'd collect the rest in full upon successful completion of the assignment. A month deadline was imposed. Titan/Hutt would keep her under watch.

Landon schooled her on the specifics of the undertaking and outlined explicit instructions relating to it. She was to follow his checklist to the letter. He stressed the importance of her behavior that would necessitate her to act normal so as not to arouse suspicions amongst her family, friends, or co-workers. No lavish or extravagant spending, even though cash would be plentiful now. No paper trail meant a temporary halt of large credit card purchases. No record or tracing of her communication to their offices could be in any computer's cache or archive. Pay phones were to be the means of contact, and only if emergently necessary. Caution of her surroundings and being followed were equally as important, crucial even. Finally, she was to confide in no one about the assignment and would return in one week to give an update. A simple nod of her head signified her understanding of his directives.

Maccabeus arose from his desk and tugged at a hinged Cezanne on a side wall that concealed a safe. He removed a stack of bills and placed them on the desk, sorting them by fifty and one hundred-dollar denominations. Funds were distributed. Her new covert mission had now been solidified. She entered into the quid pro quo agreement with trepidation, having now become a pawn in the Titan/Hutt dynasty.

Their short meeting ended with the shaking of hands and a wary smile from Miss America. She would be kept under twenty-four-hour surveillance upon leaving their offices, unawares. And also unbeknownst to her, she would not be able to voluntarily defect from her newly formed alliance with Titan/Hutt Industries, Inc.

CHAPTER THIRTEEN

Blessed Assurance

Sundays in Royalton were hallowed and revered. It was a God-fearing community, and one that gave The Almighty his due on this most sacred day of the week. Many of Royalton's forty-thousand-plus residents found themselves in a place of worship on this day. Most of the business establishments were closed, virtually shutting down the city, the exception being an occasional convenience store or local eatery. The community could easily be mistaken for a ghost town during the eleven o'clock AM hour on Sunday mornings. Jace and Perry were not members of any congregation in Royalton and did not claim any specific religious affiliation. Perry, being brought up in the church, was a faithful attendee as a child and adolescent, partly because his grandfather was a minister. Being preacher's kids meant that he and his siblings were held to a higher moral standard than the other local kids, their lives placed under a microscope and scrutinized for any lapse in moral rectitude.

Perry came to resent this infringement on his lifestyle and the judgement that came with it. Labeled a sinner and condemned to Hell, and as the years went by and he got older, he began a gradual weaning of the weekly ritual that would eventually carry over into his adulthood. Those of the religious order did not embrace the move, one in which they viewed as secular. Subsequently, the 'sisters' of his local church back home soon organized a prayer meeting for him, the prodigal *grand*son, with the idea being to pray him back to the 'fold.' Perry had strong and opinionated views on religion and the church that would foster many heated debates to anyone who boldly enter the arena with him. He saw it as a fine institution, one deserving and worthy of respect. Religion itself was never brought into question, rather the hundreds of thousands of those who embraced its philosophy and teachings, for many whose lives were not patterned accordingly. It was in his freshman year of college, and an English term paper on the very topic that would forever persuade his thinking of the religious institution.

He would visit an independent church where he was a virtual unknown to conduct research. His experience was a fascinating one that begged to be told over and over. Having been reminded again by Jace, he gave birth to the story once more:

"Sitting on my blessed *assurance* in the New Strangers Rest Fellowship of Believers Pentecostal Church," he began, "I panned the pews and eyed the faces of those who were assembled for their morning worship.

As the lengthy church name gave testament to, there were many strangers gathered for their spiritual rejuvenating, and I needed lots of rest from my last night's outing the previous evening. My reason for being in attendance was an English term paper on religion and the church. Once inside the sanctuary, I staked out an end seat on a pew near the front. I wondered why the spot was left vacant, as it offered a prime view of the proceedings ahead. An usher tried diverting me from the seat in question, and quickly stepped away at my insistence on taking it. Eyes darted at me as I claimed the spot as my own. Whisperings and nervous rustling infused the congregation as they made subtle gestures toward me, the stranger in their midst. I, the sinner, sat in the company of believers after a hard night of partying, while they sought to win as many lost souls to the 'fold' as possible. With the revered Second Coming perpetually near, they had a voracious appetite for the sin-sick, such as myself. I was not an avid churchgoer, but a believer nonetheless; of what, I wasn't quite sure. It seemed a popular thing to be at that exact moment, so I believed. A woman known as Sister Ethylene Henshaw, who, as the program read, was the head missionary of the church, made her way to my pew and stood glaring down at me as though some trespass had been made upon her property. She wore a grand hat, larger than any other bedecking the heads of the hat-wearing hens in the sanctuary. It was embellished with feathers, fruit and flowers, and a dove in-flight to complete her crowning glory. It also obstructed the view of the worshipers sitting directly behind her. She arrived late and made an opera diva entrance to the same spot she had undoubtedly sat in for years, unchallenged by the other members, but that I now occupied.

'My spot,' she sniped indignantly, while standing tall over me waiting for *her* seat to be relinquished. I twisted myself around and searched the pew for an engraved carving or metal plate bearing her name claiming the spot as hers. Not finding one, I refused to surrender the seat. She shoved her overwhelming person between me and the pew ahead and plopped down next to me, notably perturbed at what she likely perceived as my lack of respect. She had presumably struck fear in the hearts of the church members, for no one dared enter into the 'lair' of the 'lioness,' as if longevity had granted her reserved parking status within the hallowed walls of the sanctuary. And so there I was in the missionary's position waiting for the climax of the service to begin.

It was nearing eleven o'clock, the start time for morning worship. A misfit bunch of choir members filed onto the risers just behind the pulpit. Some wore robes, some did not. Others wore robes of an earlier day that did not match those of the current. Reading from the program, The Right Reverend Doctor Kymp would be presiding over the service. Exactly what was he *right* about, I began to wonder. A very tired and haggard-looking elderly female shuffled to the piano and began to offer soft music that sometimes went off key. The Right Reverend emerged from a side door followed by an entourage of 'yes' men, and took his seat in the dominant chair of the pulpit. He panned the sanctuary faces from his elevated platform and looked down upon me sitting in the 'den' of the 'big cat,' smiling at me in congratulatory success. The congregation seemed to breathe a sigh of relief at one so bold as to challenge the 'predator.' A wiry gentleman took the place of the elderly woman at the piano. The believers jumped to their feet as he began to play an up-beat congregational number that sent them into a Holy Ghost fit of singing, clapping, and dancing. *Just like last night,* I remembered. The Reverend Doctor leapt from his chair with a raised finger and proclaimed, 'Let everything that hath breath, praise the Lord!' *And let everything that hath bad breath not partake in the praising,* I thought, sitting next to Ethylene, whose breath reeked of bourbon and potted meat. The Lord, if He could smell, should not be made to suffer from her morning nightcap and missed brushing. As fate would have it, she praised the loudest, saturating the confined air with her revolting mouth fumes. 'Make a joyful noise unto the Lord...,' Reverend Kymp continued, quoting from Psalms 100.

Being filled with the spirit, Sister Ethylene began an incessant clapping of her hands. The noise was anything but joyful, nerve-wracking in my near hung-over state. Thoughts of a guillotine slicing down on her wrists entered my mind, while I waited for the jarring to cease. Visions of her now sitting there, clunking the two nubs together, tickled me as I fought to restrain an outburst of laughter. The Reverend Doctor's services could have been better served in a hospital emergency ward, rather than inciting a religious riot that would serve only to worsen my impending headache. With the praise party over, Doctor Kymp assumed his position at the podium and began to preach on the wiles of Satan's syrup. At that instant, Madam Henshaw immediately arose from her seat, raised a ceremonial index finger and tipped out of the sanctuary, making a convenient exit. The highlight of the service and my main reason for attending was the monthly laying on of hands in order to heal the sick, exorcise the demonic and uplift the afflicted. It was this portion of the service that convinced me on selecting New Strangers Rest to do research for my term paper. A first-hand account of the proceedings would increase my chances of scoring an A in class, and give my grade point average a much-needed boost. I sat through the Reverend's rather tedious discourse, anxiously awaiting the hands laying. His sermon ended after what seemed a relentless duration of time.

There was a brief period of inactivity from the pulpit. After which, the sanctuary lights were dimmed and sequential silence fell over the congregation. Bouncer-like ushers manned the exits to dissuade anyone from leaving or entering. 'It' was about to begin. From the rear of the sanctuary, a disheveled woman with dirty hair and stained teeth was escorted down the aisle to the altar. I stared Satan in the face as she gimped past my pew, making obscene gestures and indiscernible noises. Reverend Kymp stood resolute at the altar with a crucifix draped about his neck awaiting his bout with the Devil's advocate. The woman reached the pulpit and stood there, seemingly undaunted by the presence of God or His ambassador. Reverend Kymp peered into the depths of Hell as the demon glared him in the face with a welcoming challenge and an inhumane gaze, suggesting it was not of this world. It would be a reluctant adversary. The Right Reverend slapped a palmed hand on the woman's forehead, and uttered words of an unknown tongue. The devil woman stood there unyielding, as if protected by a metal coat of armor. Kymp's muddled incantations became more ominous as his voice seemed to take on a possession of its own. His eyes clenched shut.

Beaded perspiration drenched his face. His jugular veins engorged against the preacher collar around his neck. The lights were dimmed further, to the point of almost being out completely. Lit altar candles added to the already portentous mood of the proceedings. The Reverend's efforts, so far, had been disturbingly ineffectual at defeating the evil presence. The unwavering demon seed endured The Reverend's supplications to God, like some resistant strain of a deadly virus. Then suddenly, as quickly as it had appeared, the tension instantaneously left Kymp's face. He took a handkerchief from his pocket, wiped his brow and opened his eyes. The she-devil smirked at him in triumph. Reverend Kymp, too, gave a celebrated smile, as if suddenly having an epiphany from The Most High. An intricately detailed wooden pedestal stood in the far corner of the pulpit. Cradled at its top was an ornate ceramic bowl. The devil woman gave a sharp turn of her head toward the pedestal, and then cut back to the Reverend's face. The possession within became unsettled, causing a twitching of her body at Kymp's realization of the bowl and its purifying content. The Reverend Doctor advanced toward the pedestal and prayed over it. Strong men moved around the altar to encircle the possessed woman. The Reverend dipped a hand inside the bowl and stepped down from the raised platform to her. The entity became hellishly combative at his approach with the 'acid' wet on his fingers and trailing down his forearm. Deacons rushed to contain her. She began a contortion of her body in such a manner as to dislocate a joint in an attempt to free herself from their vice-like grip. Reverend Kymp reached the devil and gave a swift whip of his arm, splattering her with the Holy water. The demonic woman gnashed her teeth and chewed her tongue, while a stream of yellow liquid flowed down her leg and pooled on the sanctuary floor that had already been draped with heavy-duty plastic in contingency. Her mouth foamed red from her self-inflicted mutilation. The distressed cry of captured prey and blood-curdling roar of a lion wailed from her lungs before she collapsed in the men's arms. It was followed by a bout of dysentery that rivaled Ethylene's breath. The devil woman was hastily ushered out of the sanctuary, leaving the congregation dumbfounded. I sat in awe, and quickly realized there were forces at work far beyond those of human control.

The offertory was next on the Order of Service. The congregation sat patiently as brilliant, gold-plated collection plates, lined with red felt interior bottoms, were produced by the church deacons. The menfolk reached for their wallets, while the women dug deep into their purses to deposit their allocated ten-percent wage earnings, as the tithing receptacles were passed from one member to the next. Ushers stood at each end of the pews and kept a watchful eye over the tithing, suspicious of any hand that dipped back into the pot to break a bill or to make change. God loves a cheerful giver, I remember reading somewhere in scripture, and I cheerfully gave. Sister Ethylene had tipped back into the sanctuary from her impromptu exit prior to the sermon but after the offertory, and just minutes before the end of the service. Given the distraction of the demonic woman, I had since forgotten about our earlier tiff over who sat where. I slid down on the pew, allowing her to reclaim her domain. She smiled at me approvingly as if having been victorious over some dueling combat.

The congregation joined hands for the benediction after singing a chorus of the doxology. The service ended, and was followed by fellowship in the dining hall. The former she-devil sat calmly at a table, having been cleaned up and made present-able to the viewing public, and unaware of her transformation. Reverend Kymp greeted the parishioners at the door. He gave me a firm and almost painful handshake and invited me to visit again, perhaps even join. I acknowledged his request with a gleeful 'will do,' secured my note tablet and Bible and left the building. In the parking lot, I sat in my car reflecting on the service, bringing to memory the lyrics of the old familiar hymn *How Great Thou Art*, and recalling the thought-provoking question that Jesus' disciples asked on the angry sea: 'Who is this man, that even the wind and the waves obey him?' *Indeed!*"

Jace was tickled by the telling of the story and its dou-ble-entendre connotation. Perry delighted in sharing the expe-rience with him, further strengthening the connection already forming between them.

The paper scored its expected A. Perry left New Strangers Rest that Sunday with renewed conviction, mindful of his own personal struggle, not unlike that of Reverend Kymp and the possessed woman; a struggle that could stand to threaten the bond of friendship that he now shared with Jace, if revealed.

CHAPTER FOURTEEN

A Tapping at the Door

Jace had self-proclaimed Saturday as laundry day at their apartment. He found himself sorting through and separating their dirty clothes from the bathroom hamper of a week's worth of laundry and readying it for wash; whites, darks, and colors each being tossed into their respective piles. He emptied their shirt and pants pockets of loose coins, worn sticks of gum, old receipts, and on the rare occasion, a dollar bill or two. Perry's contribution to their clothes-care regimen was to fold them and included the arduous task of mating socks. He was napping soundly in his room. A light tapping at the door awakened him. He opened it to Jace standing there holding a small slip of paper. He could hear the rumble of the washing machine from the utility closet and suddenly realized the reason for the tapping. *Saturday*, he remembered—*laundry day*. With the pile of clothes to be washed were his plaid, retro pants, dirty from the perspiration of dancing at *Mussolini's*, and evidence from their dinner with Haley and Karter at the restaurant. He braced himself for the ensuing interrogation.

"Who's Bristol?" Jace questioned, handing Perry the slip of paper. He had forgotten. Perry reminded him of the date with Haley and Karter and their dinner at the restaurant. Jace suddenly had a vivid recollection from their then overly attentive waiter.

"What does he want?" he asked.

"I dunno," Perry answered, "he just gave me his number."

"I see," Jace stated accusingly. "So why didn't you tell me?"

"*Tell you*? Tell you what?"

"*What* do you think?" Jace snarled.

"I think you're being a little silly," Perry chuckled, but at the same time taking the offensive.

"Don't be a smart ass!" Jace rebuked.

"Sir, he gave me his number at the restaurant. Is there a problem? I see no harm in that," Perry replied.

"Yeah, well, you wouldn't," Jace sniped back.

"What's *that* supposed to mean, in fact, what's it to you anyway?" Perry countered. Jace was taken aback, then mumbled something indiscernible about the smiley face.

"Did you call him?" he asked Perry.

"No."

"Are you going to?"

"Sure, why wouldn't I?"

"Why would you?" Jace demanded. It was a valid question; one Perry didn't have an answer to.

He and Jace practically did everything together and were virtually inseparable. They had no secrets, or so Jace thought. "Bristol would threaten our friendship," he would later confess.

Perry came to the realization that the bond building between them was suddenly becoming not so one-sided anymore. In a remorseful gesture, he took the slip of paper, ripped it into tiny pieces and trashed them. Jace turned and walked off without saying another word. Their heated exchange was the closest they had ever come to any kind of discord. It seemed trivial and left them both feeling regretful. Perry was filled with an overwhelming desire to embrace him and apologize. He would at least apologize. Jace had retreated to the living room. He sat on the sofa, remote in hand, surfing through the television channels. Perry stood leaning against the wall, his presence obvious. Jace clicked off the television and glanced over at him. His expression suggested hurt and disappointment. In an attempt at redeeming himself, Perry played his one and only trump card, the one about Jace's employment at the Royalton office and how he was responsible for it. It was a long shot and had little effect. Jace said he figured as much, knowing full well his review from corporate would not be favorable.

"I knew when we first met and shook hands that you would come to my defense," he told Perry, and voiced his gratitude.

"Anything for you," Perry muttered under his breath and to himself, but that Jace also heard.

"Sorry for being a smart-ass earlier," Perry finally mustered the nerve to say.

"It's okay," Jace reassured. Perry joined him on the sofa. They stared at the blank screen and said little. Jace positioned himself on the sofa facing Perry. He clutched one of the accent pillow cushions, his legs crossed beneath him.

"How did your mom die?" Jace asked. Perry was caught off guard. His family had never been a topic of discussion between them. He avoided it. He pondered the origin of Jace's question, yet another he did not have an answer to. Had Trudy put him up to it? He wondered. Perry knew that his reluctance in openly discussing his family served only to pique her curiosity, sensing she was never completely satisfied with his ambiguous answers in response to her broaching the subject. Yes, she had put him up to it, he was sure of it. Many times in his thirty-plus years, he had been asked this same question. His response was always a perplexed, 'I don't know.' He offered it again. His grandfathers had taken the cause to the grave with them, while his grandmother would break down in a torrent of tears when probed. He would not ask her again.

She, too, would bury it with her. Older siblings feigned ignorance and passed the buck on to the eldest, who in turn, bounced it back to the underlings after him. He felt alienated from his dad's side of the family and would not tread the delicate matter with them. 'Take care of my children,' were his mother's last spoken words, told to his maternal grandmother. It was the only shared insight of her death. The cause became suspect. Perry vowed to return home unannounced, pay a visit to the county courthouse, and obtain her death certificate. To date, he had not. His procrastination for not having done so was a fear of the unknown.

With no one in the family willing to talk about it, he began to imagine all kinds of ideas as to how she had died. Everything from a freak accident to some medical malady entertained his thoughts, though neither of those warranted the hush-hush from his family. He became saddened and turned away from Jace to hide his watering eyes. Jace moved toward him to console and now sat very close at his side. A single tear trickled down Perry's cheek as he focused on a framed eight-by-ten of his mother smiling warmly at him from a corner shelf. In an instance of vulnerability, he laid his head on Jace's shoulder as he tried to stifle further tears. Jace responded by placing an arm around him. He rested his chin atop Perry's head and gave him a gentle squeeze. "It's okay," he whispered softly. "It's okay." Next week, Perry decided he would return home. He had some lingering reservations about the idea, fearing it might unleash a legion of woes. He kept them to himself. Jace would make the journey with him. They both dozed off.

The obnoxious yelp of a car alarm blared from the parking lot and awakened them. Startled, they jumped from their positions on the sofa. Jace rushed to the window to investigate, relieved that his beloved sports car was not the source of the disturbance. He took great pride in the vehicle, never letting it collect more than a thin layer of dust before driving it off to the carwash. Perry thought it a bit compulsive. Until recent, the car had been Jace's primary focus. It was dependable and always there when needed, much like the friend he had found in Perry. Perry hoped it would only be a matter of time before Jace would come to realize it.

CHAPTER FIFTEEN

Good vs. Evil

The car was followed from a distance. Her story of how she had acquired the new vehicle, given her financial woes, didn't add up. Miss America was weaving a web of tangled lies that left many unanswered questions and heightened suspicions of her behavior. Her explanation of the wig and video discovered in her duffle bag didn't wash either. She became irritable when questioned about them. There was no other alternative but this recourse for those closest to her. Speeding along the freeway at speeds of more than seventy miles per hour, the hired private investigator failed to notice the black car trailing him as he followed her. She took a north exit ramp leading into the Bayou City, the two-car convoy in pursuit. They weaved their way through a series of flyovers and traffic congestion on the Beltway. Nearing downtown, a sudden jolt propelled the investigator's car abruptly forward, the seatbelt locking him in place preventing an impact with the steering wheel and windshield. Looking in his rear-view mirror, he noticed a black SUV had struck his vehicle from behind. They took the next exit off the freeway and pulled onto a side street.

She continued into downtown. The investigator slammed his hands on the steering wheel in disgust and got out of the car. A nicely dressed gentleman in a business suit met him at the trunk and offered a convincing apology while they assessed the damage. After the exchange of automobile and insurance information, and with some stalling on his part, Landon made a quick escape and hurried to downtown, making sure he was not being followed.

She was waiting for him in the office tower atrium, wearing the same long, brunette hair, swathed in a scarf, and dark pointed sunglasses, looking very sophisticated and every bit of belonging. She glanced over at a towering marble clock in the center of the atrium. He was not there at their scheduled time. She became paranoid and left the sunglasses on to deter anyone from talking to her. Maccabeus was waiting for them on the seventy-fifth floor. They were already late. Efficiency was hallowed at Titan/Hutt. He would not be pleased with their tardiness. But she had been careless and unobservant. He would understand. If the diversion on the freeway had not been created, their plot to extinguish the attorney may have been discovered and the mission foiled.

Given this circumstance, their tardiness would be forgivable, Landon reasoned. Her extravagant spending on her pauper income was arousing suspicions. It was careless of her to buy the new car at the onset of the assignment; questions were being asked, and she had been warned. Compounding matters was her lack of situational awareness in being followed, another prospect she'd been cautioned of. She was becoming a liability for Hutt. No, he would not be pleased. It was strike one for Miss America.

Landon arrived and met her in the atrium as planned. He apologized for being late and keeping her waiting. They hurried to the elevator for the ascent as he told a reconstructed account of the accident. Stopping briefly by his office on the seventieth floor, they witnessed the wrath of Olive, the Mrs. Maccabeus Hutt, his mother. A woman of girth with unruly breasts and short on patience, she barked out orders from an estrogen-induced tirade that sent employees scampering to satisfy her every whim. She liked giving the impression of being a key player in the decision-making at her husband's company, when, in actuality, her tirades stemmed from that of mere tidiness only. Sharing no part in the day-to-day running of the Titan/Hutt enterprise, she made her monthly stomp through the offices, created a disturbance, then was off to afternoon tea with one of her socialite hags of new money fame. Maccabeus forbade her to visit more than once a month. Landon would not openly lay claim to her.

Miss America and Maccabeus were meeting for the second time. He listened intently as she detailed her betrayal by way of an 'accidental' tragedy that would soon befall the attorney. She enlisted his help for the plan. It was a clever plot, brilliant almost. Maccabeus was excitedly pleased at the well thought out scheme. He assured that any resource needed for the plan was at her disposal, sweet vindication from her impetuous care-lessness. She was smugly proud of herself at his delight. Dollar signs danced in her head as all sense of reasoning and rational-ity left her. Her judgment became impaired by the prospect of fast and easy money. The forces of good and evil were at war with Miss America. Evil reared its ugly head, lending credence to the belief that money was the root of it all. It had prevailed. She had stooped to the very lowest of morality and left his office again a wealthier woman.

He was known only to her as "Dobbs." Brakes, or the absence of, were his specialty. Mr. Coffey would be going by his old office to gather some personal belongings and have lunch with a few of the partners. Dobbs would be patiently awaiting his arrival on level ten of the parking garage. He would disable the attorney's car's braking system at the designated speed and disengage the seatbelt mechanism.

Forecasters were predicting another rainy day, complete with slick streets and the possibility of dense fog. Miss America thought it the opportune time for an accidental collision. She knew and mapped out the routing he would take from the office back to Galatian Avenue. The brakes would fail at a 'T' intersection facing a concrete wall memorial. He would be trav-eling on the north and south thoroughfare of the 'T.' From prior car trips with him, she knew he had a 'lead' foot. The wet streets and dense fog would add salt to an already open wound and exacerbate the now increasingly dismal scheme. A slam into the concrete wall at accelerated speed would inflict massive musculo-skeletal trauma and bleeding, and wreak a havoc of internal injuries not compatible with life.

CHAPTER SIXTEEN

Discovery

They rented a car for the drive to Perry's hometown. The bulk of the trip would be in Texas and getting out of the state. They would alternate at the wheel every hundred miles or so. The trip would bring finality and closure surrounding the mystery and secrecy of his mother's death. Jace questioned if Perry were mentally prepared to handle the discovery, be it good or bad.

"Regardless of the cause," Perry told him, "You'll be with me." Jace smiled and seemed to delight in the knowledge that someone found reassurance in him, something lacking in his marriage. During the drive, they reminisced and shared stories of their youth. Perry gave an outlandish account of how he, as a child, had a vivid recollection of the drive-thru carwash down at the local gas station. He referred to it as the metal-eating monster to which he was wonderfully afraid:

"It sat pompously in the corner of the gas station parking lot, awaiting its next meal of metal, glass, and rubber. My uncle would challenge the creature with each fill-up visit. At the entrance of the monster's mouth, its Cyclops eye stared us down and blinked from red to green, signaling the start of the onslaught. It then swallowed us whole. I screamed. Once inside the monster's mouth, its salivary glands excreted a foamy substance to paralyze and keep us still. It worked every time because I could feel the car running but we weren't going anywhere. Then, its vicious assault began. I held a hand over my eyes with my middle and index fingers slightly parted to witness the bloodletting. Its massive, severed tongue swept over the car many times, sending it rocking back and forth. The monster hadn't noticed us inside, yet. All was quiet and still, when suddenly, piercing jets of spittle rained down on the car's exterior. I never fully understood why. The assault lasted all of five minutes and was over. The monster then spat us out, dissatisfied with our taste, I supposed. I would get out to inspect the car, only to find it to be remarkably clean, with no evidence of trauma or abuse. My uncle, unfazed by the whole experience, would then drive off on our merry way, smiling to himself all the while."

Jace bolted with laughter at what he called, "An absolute ridiculous story."

"It wasn't so 'ridiculous' at the time," Perry replied, almost offended.

"Only from the mind of a child," Jace stated. It *was* pretty ridiculous, Perry admitted.

They crossed the Texas state border just after midnight. Within the hour, they arrived in Perry's hometown and checked into a cheap motel. They were both exhausted. In the morning, they would visit the county courthouse.

Morning came, and with it, anxiety for Perry. Sleep did not come easy for him. He had tossed and turned much of the night, stressing over the discovery they were about to make. Was it really that important? He began to have his doubts. His family seemed at peace with the matter, why shouldn't he? He asked himself. Jace had slept soundly during the night and was completely refreshed by morning. Perry did not share his anxieties with him but moved about the motel room in a zombie-like state. The two friends found themselves squeezed into the cramped space of the small bathroom readying for the day. Jace was at the sink shaving, a towel draped loosely around his waist. Perry stood statuesque in the shower, deep in thought, as the tepid water rained over his naked and motionless body. His eyes were closed. Jace watched him in the mirror through the translucent shower curtain, somehow sensing his angst. Perry's trance-like state was broken by the sound of a familiar voice calling him. He jumped upon hearing Jace and leaned over to turn off the water.

"You okay?" Jace asked. Perry answered him with an unconvincing, "Yeah." He slid the shower curtain back and reached for a towel. Jace was wearing the last one, the other being used

as a floor mat. Only a small washcloth hung on the towel railing. Perry stepped out of the shower and onto the towel with
Jace to avoid the cold floor, his body still dripping with water.
Jace moved to allow him room, but remained on the
towel. Their eyes met in an unspoken 'now what' stare. Jace
removed the towel from around his waist and handed it to
Perry. Perry dried himself, then wrapped the towel back
around Jace's naked body. They finished their morning ritual
of shaving, brushing, and showering. Perry reached around
Jace to the hook on the bathroom door for his True Religions
and slid them on over his bare bottom. He donned a ball cap,
pulling the brim low on his forehead to avoid recognition.

They took the stairs down to the lobby to assess the complimentary, continental breakfast items. Perry took one bite out
of a bagel spread with cream cheese and made a mad dash to
the bathroom, determining that food would not be agreeable
with him in his anxious state. Jace grabbed a pecan roll and
seven-up, handing the soda to Perry for his nervous stomach.
They left the motel and headed for the courthouse.

The county courthouse was an impressive and intimidat-
ing structure, an architectural feat at the time of its construction over one hundred years ago. Solidly built of limestone
and threateningly beautiful, the building had the appearance
of a medieval castle, with its towering spires and grotesquely
gargoyles extending from its carved-out niches in a protective
watch over the town. Here, in this great edifice where justice
was dispensed, were decades of birth records, death certificates,
marriage licenses, divorce decrees, voter registrations, criminal

histories and traffic violations. The two friends stood outside admiring the imposing structure with its pristine landscaping and daring welcoming. They traversed its lush lawn, that was parted by a wide sidewalk and climbed up the steep limestone steps, lined with brass hand railings, to the lobby entrance. Inside, the glossy, terrazzo floors gave off a wavy and hypnotizing reflection that did not settle well on Perry's already queasy stomach. The stately appointments and armed guards served only to worsen his anxiety. Another bathroom visit beckoned him while Jace waited outside the MENS door. Perry emerged and they made their way to the reception desk. A middle-aged woman behind the counter looked up from her busying and greeted them.

"Good morning," she said, overtly cheerful for the time of day. It nauseated Perry even more. "Can I help you?" she asked. They told her the purpose of their visit and she sprang into action. Perry wanted to go home and forget all about his notion of knowing.

The clerk escorted them down a long hall to a large open room of metal cabinets drawers, hanging files, and slotted counters. After telling her a month and year, she produced a cumbersome binder and plopped it on the counter. Dust wafted from its pages. Jace settled the seven-dollar certificate fee, then she darted off. 1969 was not a good year to be alive, as it had claimed many in its passing, judging by the thickness of the binder.

Perry's heart raced as he flipped the pages that were not in the best of alphabetical order. He took great care not to rip the already worn pages with each turn. He didn't want to be there. 'Let sleeping dogs lie,' he recalled an older brother telling him at his persistence in knowing. Maybe he was right, Perry conceded. He continued turning the pages, stopping to read the misfortunes of others in the sixty-ninth year and prolonging the inevitable. Jace stood over his shoulder watching intently and fidgeted at his delay. Perry gave another cautious flip of a page. There, at the top, his mother's name—Billie Lane St. Kane. It gave him pause. He stared at it as though hypnotized. Jace rested a hand on his shoulder. Perry examined the certificate. Near the bottom read CAUSE OF DEATH, his palm pressed firmly over it. They had come this far and now he didn't want to know. Jace pried his hand away and studied the document for an extended period.

"Don't tell me!" Perry shouted at him. "Don't tell me."

"Shhh!" Jace gestured, with an index finger at his pursed lips. Others in the archival room stopped their searching and stared at them with inquisitive faces. An armed guard was making his way in their direction.

"Let's go," Perry demanded, grabbing Jace by the arm.

"What about…?" Jace started to ask.

"Leave it," Perry interrupted.

"But we've come this…" Jace stuttered.

"Leave it," Perry snapped again, pulling him toward the exit. The clerk sat at her position and glared at them with furrowed eyebrows as they left the building.

It was noon, checkout time. They spoke all of ten words on the return drive, stopping only to eat. Perry knew that Jace wanted to speak but hoped he wouldn't. Jace didn't press the obvious. He reclined in the passenger seat and slept for the better part of the drive. Perry glanced over at him and wondered what information he had seen and read. At another time and place would he allow Jace to share in the knowledge of the discovery. He exceeded the speed limit until crossing the border back into Texas. Jace awakened to complete the drive.

Back home it was business as usual.

CHAPTER SEVENTEEN

The Error of Ways

"9-1-1, what is your emergency?"

"My brakes are kaput."

The operator, "Excuse me?"

"My brakes have gone out, woman!"

With urgency in her voice, the operator asks, "Are you driving now? You can't stop your vehicle?"

"Both," replied the calm voice from the other end.

"Well, which is it?" she asked.

"*Yes*, I'm driving now, and *no*, I can't stop my vehicle. *Both, Bitch*," the now irritated caller answered.

"I beg your pardon!" she snapped indignantly.

"And I beg to differ," the caller rebuffed.

"What, who are you? Is this a prank?"

"No, it's a call for help. Seems I got the wrong number."

"This is 9-1-1. What is your emergency?"

"You said that already."

"DO YOU HAVE AN EMERGENCY?" the operator demanded. There was no response.

"Hello? Where are you?" she asked.

"Parking lot of the mall, as if you give a good got damn."

"Are there any other vehicles around?"

"Only the ones I'm gittin' ready to annihilate," a child's voiced suddenly giggled.

"How fast are you going?"

"CHOO-CHOOO!" yelled the voice from the other end.

"Ok, how much gas do you have?"

"I passed it already, lady," came a broken and static reply. The operator gave instruction to turn off the ignition. Once again, there was no response. The connection was lost. She dispatched an engine to the mall.

The fire department arrived to find the driver in a whirlwind of hurried revolutions to nowhere. He is on a mobile phone, seemingly unnerved by his brake system failure. Grinning, he waves at the firemen as he passes by them with each speedy revolve. They unsuccessfully yell at him to turn off the ignition. He does not hear. With their arms simulating that of a cranking motion, the firemen attempt to get him to roll down the window. Thinking they are making obscene gestures at him, 'Junior' extends his middle finger as the others curl simultaneously downward and yells back at them, "UP YOURS BUDDY!" The firemen were stupefied. "AND YA MAMA'S TOO," he continued. Meanwhile, a phone call was made to the home on Galatian Avenue. Trudy's busying about the kitchen was interrupted by the ringing phone. She wiped her hands on a nearby dish towel and reached for the receiver.

"Hello?" she answered on the first ring. Dead air filled her ear, followed by a child's snicker.

"Eugene?" she asked, with an air of suspicion in her voice. After receiving no answer, but being relatively certain of her mysterious caller's identity, she authoritatively informed, "This is your mother, Eugene."

"Yes, Ma'am?" the 'boy' answered with drawling utterance and defeat.

"What's going on?" she asked him.

"I was playin' the game first and they'll just have to wait their turn," the 'boy' said. "NO CUTTIN' IN LINE!" she heard him yell away from the phone.

"They who?" she asked.

"The other conductors in their funny yellow coveralls and red suspenders. They wanna play too, Mama," he answered. Trudy could hear the pleas from the firemen over the phone. *Turn it off. Turn it off,* they shouted.

"Wait yer turn," Junior snapped again. Realizing she would never get to the gist of what was going on from talking to her husband-boy, she followed the pursuit of the firemen.

"It's time to turn off the game, Eugene," she calmly stated, but with firm intention.

"But Maaa," he whined.

"NOW! Eugene. Turn it OFF!" Fearing some grave consequence, he grasped the key and twisted it back.

The car jerked to a sudden stop, thrusting him forward and then slamming him back against the seat. The firemen rushed the car and unlocked the door from the now rolled down driver's window.

"Sir, are you all right?" a fireman asked. He did not answer.

"Sir?" the fireman repeated, trying to elicit a response from the pouty lips-looking occupant.

"Shut up, dickwad, I heard ya the first time," 'Junior' huffed.

"Well why didn't you say so?" the fireman snapped back.

Junior glared at him and said, "Of course I'm alright. You ain't the sharpest knife in the drawer, are ya?"

Trudy's muffled voiced could be heard from the cell phone. Like a petulant child, her husband-son held it clenched in his fist and refused to let go. Attempts to retrieve the phone were met with combativeness as he punched at the firemen's hands while they tried to pry the phone away.

"Sir, we just want to speak with someone about coming to get you," one of the firemen stated, while struggling with him for the cell phone.

"Oh, I'm sorry, I didn't mean to insult your lack of intelligence, dumb-nuts," Mr. Coffey's alter ego sneered.

Irritated and wet from the rain, the fireman refused to speak to him further. Trudy arrived at the scene to claim her juvenile husband. She offered a brief explanation to the firemen and made her apologies.

The car was towed to a nearby service center. After a thorough inspection, the technician reported the brakes to be in perfect working condition. Though puzzled by the disengagement, he repaired the system and seatbelt mechanism and reported the car safe to drive again. His stamp of approval was of little comfort to Trudy. They had had the car for almost a decade. Considering what had just happened, and the dead battery incident in the parking garage, she decided it was time to retire the vehicle. Mr. Coffey revolted but to no avail. He absolutely cherished the car and was faithful to it. It had been good to him, not one significant breakdown in the nearly ten years of ownership, the reason for keeping it as long as they had. He would instead have to use her car for his simple errands around town. Trudy would not permit him to venture beyond the city limits and would now restrict his travels to within a few blocks of their home. This did not sit well with him. He would sometimes drive to the outskirts of town in defiance of her and gaze out at the horizon of the forbidden world before him. That made him feel better.

She had an unspoken fear of Maccabeus. Her plan had failed. He would not be pleased. The imposed deadline was nearing. *Why had he gone home a different way?* She wondered. Miss America again found herself speeding along on the Beltway, racing toward downtown Houston. She had been summoned to the Titan/Hutt offices. There were matters of importance to be discussed. Specifically, her next strategy; plan B as it were. Maccabeus was quickly losing patience; but Miss America wanted no further involvement in the plot to extinguish the attorney. She sat nervously in the chair across from his massive desk voicing her desire to end their agreement. She wanted out. Maccabeus looked at her with a raised eyebrow and deceitful grin. He chuckled at the notion that she 'wanted out.'

"Quid pro quo," he spoke, almost inaudibly. He had already paid out thousands to her. She was now living a comfortable life *because* of him. Where was the appreciation? He couldn't help but ask himself. He pressed on the sides of his forehead, and then brought his palms together to his lips as if in prayer.

"Quid pro quo," he whispered again, while now lightly tapping the tips of his fingers together, contemplative.

They had an agreement. There was no stored record of their pact that he could retrieve as a means of reminding her; nothing committed to pen and paper bearing her signature as to provide evidence of her full knowledge, consent and participation. Maccabeus was undaunted by this prospect. It was a verbal understanding between the two of them. She had not produced. The desired effect had not been met. There was still a debt to be paid. It was what brought her here in the first place, *debt* freedom. But her plan had backfired. She now realized the error of her ways, but at what cost. Betrayal? Riches? Death? Maccabeus gave her request a fleeting thought, never seriously considering it. *No*, he determined. There was a 'contract' to be honored. He had done his part, more even. The very automobile which brought her to him, *he* paid for. She had brought nothing to the table. It was an audacious move on her part, one to be admired in any other facet, but not here.

How could she have known. Maccabeus pushed away from his desk in the wheeled wingback. With unhurried resolve, he stood and rounded the corner of the desk to her. A swift and powerful backhanded slap to her face sent her tumbling to the floor in the chair. He took out a handkerchief from his pocket and wiped his knuckles and mouth, while casually strolling to the bar. He prepared a cocktail and presented it to her. Her cheek glowed red from the blow, as the orbit of her eye began to fill with fluid and swell. He grabbed the back of her head, the brunette wig coming off in his hand. Tossing it aside, he bent over and whispered menacingly, "Do it!" He then released his grip, allowing her head to drop back freely to the floor. Blood streamed from her eye, down her face, and seeped into her mouth. She became nauseated and began to retch from the taste of her own self. Maccabeus glared at her in disgust. He moved back to the desk and commenced with the task of running his operation. She, too, would have to be extinguished, he now thought. Greed had come with a price, and regret. Miss America struggled to her feet, donned the wig and pointed sunglasses and stumbled out of the office. Strike two.

CHAPTER EIGHTEEN

Ty Bo

To say Jace Coffey's wife was a bitch would be an understatement, disrespectful even without affording her the proper title of *Miss*. Perry had the unfortunate pleasure of making her acquaintance late one Monday evening. Jace needed to go by his old apartment to gather some forgotten things in the move. He asked Perry to go with him, giving advance warning of her bitter disposition. Perry agreed, but said he'd wait in the car. Jace insisted he go in with him. A phone call to the apartment received no answer, suggesting her absence. Her car was nowhere to be seen in the parking lot of the complex upon their arrival. A ring of the bell and a knock on the door was not answered. Jace had kept a spare key and was using it now. *Not a good thing*, Perry determined. Inside the apartment was the making of a happy home.

Pictures of the newly wedded couple still held their position in various places. In one, she sat nestled in his embrace, blissfully content. A testament to their everlasting love was framed and hung on the entrance wall. Atop the fireplace mantle, a bronze sculpture of our Lord and Savior commanded top billing. Her feminine influence was abundant throughout. Scented potpourri filled their nostrils with the essence of vanilla and bergamot. An amalgamation of assorted plants hung from a corner ceiling in a failed attempt at décor, reflected by a gilded Louis XV-inspired mirror. Jace took notice of items unfamiliar to him and obviously newly-acquired. He assumed the 'other' man was being financially supportive of her, as he hadn't made the extravagant purchases he now found himself surrounded by in her, rather *their* apartment. Perry studied the suspending plant jungle, trying to determine the statement it was struggling to make. In a further salute to gaudiness, ornate Roman pedestals occupied the corners of the living room, topped with busy faux flowers in gold-plated vases. While Jace shuffled through boxes in another room, Perry examined trinkets and other knick-knacks scattered around and about the living and dining areas. Nothing gave evidence to their marital strife, but further reinforced their committed devotion to one another that had long since ended. Jace appeared with a stack of papers and was ready to leave. Perry eagerly agreed. It appeared as though luck had been kind to them until they heard the rattle of keys in the front door, when in she stepped, tired, and in a foul state. Perry was smitten by her uncompromised beauty and determined that Jace had a knack for attracting beautiful women, given his wife could easily compete. It didn't take long, though, for the stressors of her day to manifest; the weight of the world, and life, heavy on her shoulders in that very moment. Jace introduced Perry. She made no acknowledgement, other than a scathing look at him. She would dislike anyone who took an interest in her soon-to-be ex-husband, including his family, innocent bystanders of their marital union that had gone horribly awry. Immediately, she questioned how he had gained entry into *her* apartment that *he* was still paying the rent on. She demanded the return of the key and threatened to call the police if he did not.

"Go ahead," Jace told her. "I have as much right to be here as you do." *Bad answer*, Perry winced, cringing at his response, and suddenly finding himself caught in the inevitable crossfire. After calling Jace everything *but* a child of God, her vehemence then shifted to Perry. "And just who the hell are you?" she barked.

"Just a friend," Perry answered meekly.

"My ass!" she snapped. At that, Jace came to Perry's defense and the fight was on. His wife turned to him and began a verbal assault that would make the devil himself scowl in disapproval. Flailing her arms wildly, she bolted toward him. Fearing another slapped cheek, Jace intercepted her swing, firmly gripping her wrist in his hand.

"Let me go!" she insisted, attempting to twist herself from his grip. He refused. Her caustic verbal assault continued. With her mouth wide open, her canines poised, she lunged toward his hand ready to bite. Jace, at that instant, released her. She then commenced to make a wreck of the apartment; the trinkets, knick-knacks, and whatnots all busted in her rabid fit. Jace moved toward Perry.

"I'll wait in the car," Perry anxiously informed, and turned to leave the apartment.

The last thing he remembered was the flying cast-iron skillet that was intended for Jace but missed its target. The white light shone incredibly bright, and for a time Perry thought he had crossed over to the other side. Where was the Right Reverend *Doctor* when he needed him, he reflected. He awoke to an emergency room physician standing over him, with a penlight aimed at his eye to gauge his pupillary response. A slight concussion and a symmetrical row of sutures to his forehead were the order of the evening. He would otherwise, be okay. Jace sat in the chair next to Perry's bed and apologized repeatedly for subjecting him to his wife's fanatical behavior and diatribe. Likewise, she, in a moment of civility, voiced a forced apology for what had occurred. She then surrendered to regretful emotions at her actions and wept uncontrollably. It was the culmination of all she had been through, with and apart from Jace; the proverbial straw that broke the camel's back, the icing on the cake. Jace went to comfort his wife, receiving no retaliation from her, though not likely a step toward reconciliation of their marriage. After Perry's discharge they parted ways. She again apologized and disappeared into the maze of cars in the parking lot.

Jace and Perry arrived home to find Ty and Bo, the weasel and boa, in a standoff. The ferret had free reign of their apartment and would oftentimes flaunt his independence at the constrictor. The boa had apparently slithered out from his unsecured glass den to experience this democracy. The loose lid on the aquarium confirmed it. Perry scooped up Ty out of harm's way. Jace wrangled Bo back into his enclosure. Perry had taken a liking to the ferret and scolded Jace for his carelessness.

"Ty can take care of himself," Jace proudly announced. Perry wasn't so convinced. Another misadventure, and Bo would become a handbag and boots, he warned and threatened. Jace chuckled at his remark and went to secure the snake.

The following day, Jace received a three-way phone call from Alex and Asher, informing him that they had been summoned home at the behest of their mother. He, too, was included in the summons, along with Perry. Something was up. There was no reason given for the impromptu visit, and the twins had no further details to share. Provident Falls was nearly a two-hour drive from Royalton, and a forty-five minute commute from the twins in Common Wells. The sibling trio could not imagine what could be so mysterious as to require their sudden presence, but deduced it had something to do with their father. *What had he done now?* They wondered.

CHAPTER NINETEEN

The Provident Events

The phone call came at 3:20 in the afternoon. It was a clear and sunny spring day. Mr. Coffey never heard the approaching train. A treat was in store for him this day. Trudy was giddy with excitement over it. She wanted the family there to share in the surprise and kept it a secret for fear of an inadvertent leak. She had seen the set up for a traveling carnival on her way home from volunteering at the Youth House. It was in, of all places, the parking lot of the mall where Mr. Coffey had his memorable encounter with the City's fire department. Of singular interest to her was a carnival train ride, complete with a caboose and conductor's seat in the lead car. The track was designed to wind its way up and over the parking lot, and advance through a dark tunnel before the ride's final lap, then end. It would be to him like a kid at Disneyland, and a celebration of him having survived his near-death experience. That was cause enough for Trudy. She made certain his coveralls and conductors cap were especially clean for his real time experience. Jace and Perry had made the drive from Royalton. The twins, along with Jessyca and Kali, were already at the house. Mr. Coffey had no knowledge of the surprise and was expected back at any minute from an errand only a few blocks away. He was late, as so often was his custom, though forgivable this occurrence. Trudy called his cell phone to check his whereabouts. It was answered after two rings. She immediately jerked the receiver away from her ear at a haunting roar on the other end. It was the three o'clock train, on schedule, as it had been for years. She stared blankly into the receiver.

In hurried excitement to get to Hammonds Collectibles for the reserved, "limited-edition" boxcar to add to his collection, Mr. Coffey would break the driving boundaries put in place by his wife. And he'd forget to put in his hearing aid. He shifted the car's gear selector to NEUTRAL, stopping to search for and insert the device, unaware the sedan had slowly rolled onto the tracks. The three o'clock train was rapidly approaching. A vibrating in his shirt pocket indicated a caller to his mobile phone. He blindly pressed the receiver icon button after the second vibration to stop the buzzing, which simultaneously answered the call, while he obliviously fumbled around the car's interior for the hearing device. Having finally retrieved it from the passenger floorboard underneath the seat, he looked up in just enough time to read the UNION PACIFIC inscription on the lead car of the speeding locomotive and flip the *on* switch of the hearing aid to the deafening roar of the freight train now bellowing in his ears, at the same time Trudy jerked the receiver away from hers.

Trudy slowly and methodically placed the receiver back in its cradle on the base of the telephone. She waited, hoping and praying for its continued silence. The shell-shocked look on her face gave clue to some awful occurrence, privy only to her, yet waiting to be revealed. She was mute to her eldest son standing before her asking repeatedly, "Mom, what's wrong?" Jace leaned over and shook her shoulder, breaking the distant gaze in her unblinking eyes.

"Mother?" he called to her again. Her blank stare focused on him, as tears began to flood her eyes. Minutes later, the phone rang with a simultaneous knock on the front door. Two, somber-faced uniformed officers stood at the entrance. They were invited inside. She already knew.

There was never a special, "limited-edition" boxcar on reserve for him at Hammonds, not now, not then—not ever. Miss America had completed the assignment. She would be rewarded handsomely, her life now spared by the loss of his. The tragedy made the front-page headline of *The Provident Events-News*:

NOTED ATTORNEY KILLED IN TRAIN CRASH!

The Falls community went into a depression. Jace, remembering his half-witted premonition in his mother's kitchen, was devastated.

A graveside ceremony in his memory overflowed with hundreds. Questions plagued the minds of the community as they struggled to understand how he had cheated death, only to be met with this fate. A lone mourner in the crowd knew the answer. Maccabeus and his entourage were in attendance. Although he and the now deceased attorney were on opposing sides, he thought it proper to show his respect and offer condolences on behalf of Titan/Hutt. A young woman standing behind him with her hair swathed in a scarf had a vague resemblance to the younger Mrs. Coffey, though it was hard to tell through the dark sunglasses she was wearing. Jace had made no mention of her attending the service. Perry stood with Jessyca and Kali directly behind the family and whispered to them as more mourners continued to file in just before the service commencement. Neither seemed interested in his idle chatter. Tensions had flared on the ride over in the limo. Kali had sparred with Asher and now refused to stand with him, fueling their already precarious relationship, and threatening to call off their wedding, permanently. Jessyca, attempting to mediate, unintentionally sided with Asher, causing a rift between her and Kali that had already been festering for reasons known only to them. Alex snapped at the trio for the inappropriateness of their bickering. Jace remained neutral. In a conciliatory gesture, Jessyca chose to stand next to Kali rather than Alex, but to also retaliate against him for his scolding of them.

The crowd settled. A clergyman was making his way to the podium. The service was about to begin. Also in attendance was William "Dobbs" Case. Back at Falls Mercy ICU, his wife had come out of her coma and was following simple commands and making purposeful movements. She had even recognized him on his visit just before the service. Maccabeus glanced down at Dobbs, giving him a subtle head nod.

A chorus of children from the Youth House sang softly in a farewell tribute to Donerson Eugene Coffey, penned by Alex, inciting a chain reaction of sniffling and watering eyes throughout the crowd:

We say goodbye to you
We say goodbye to you
Get on my passenger train
Hear what the Savior says
We say goodbye to you.

We say goodbye to you
We say goodbye to you
Get on my passenger train
I hear the Savior say
We say goodbye to you.

Standing at the coffin pit and speaking over the softly singing children's chorus, the minister uttered the all-too-familiar words heard only at such an occasion:

"Dust to dust and ashes to ashes," he spoke, while tossing flower petals from the centerpiece coffin arrangement into the six-foot excavation. The attorney's flag-draped coffin, in the shape of a boxcar, was lowered into the ground. He had served his country well. It seemed ironic that the very thing which took his life, would now preserve his death. The clergyman gave the final declaration to the attendees, bringing the service to an end:

"The Lord has given and The Lord has taken away. Blessed be the name of The Lord."

The crowd dispersed as the harmonious sound of the children's voices stayed its course.

Get on my passenger train
I hear the Savior say
We say goodbye to you.

Mrs. Coffey, stoic throughout, was burdened and very tired. The events had taken their toll, eating away at her like an ulcer. It was feared she would succumb to a nervous breakdown. Battered and bruised, she weathered the storm. Jace hadn't fared so well. Many nights would find him in Perry's room sobbing uncontrollably. The evening of the ceremony being one such night. The separation. His pending divorce and "at-will" employment. And now, his father's accident and untimely death, had all pushed him to his limit. He could take no more. A waterfall of tears streamed from his eyes. Sobs of sorrow soon filled the room. Perry held him close in bed singing softly *You'll Never Walk Alone.*

Slowly the sobs subsided. Jace rested his head on Perry's bare chest. Perry massaged his scalp and held him as Jace drifted off to sleep. Perry, too, felt himself growing tired and would soon follow suit. All was quiet and still. The flickering flame of a candle cast its shadow on the wall. Perry watched him. Jace lay sleeping peacefully, as peaceful as a newborn baby. Perry watched him.

The melody of chirping birds could be heard from the outside. A gentle breeze whistled in and parted the curtains from an open window, they danced in formation. Waves splashed upon the shore from Lake Royalton. Leaves from a nearby tree rustled the ground below, completing nature's symphony. A ray of sunlight beamed through an open window in a masterpiece work of art. Perry and Jace roused from their sleep, their arms and legs entangled in each other's. The serene morning was that of storybook and fairytale. Not speaking, they separated from one another, fully cognizant of the foreign place they now found themselves in. Alcohol was not a factor to be blamed. It was by no accident that Jace now found himself wearing only a pair of boxers. He apologized for his crying fit and, gathering his clothes, made a hasty departure from Perry's room.

CHAPTER TWENTY

Secret Things, Shattered Dreams

Kali sat staring out the bedroom window of the two-story home she shared with Asher. She was in pensive thought. It was nearing six o'clock. He would be returning home from work soon. How could she tell him? Their relationship had suffered. She didn't know what else to do. Would he understand? Could he cope? Did it matter? Her unpredictable mood swings added further strain and fanned the flames of their already tumultuous relationship. Today was especially vexing for Asher. Her insistence that nothing was wrong served only to frustrate him even more. *How could she be calm one minute and out of mind the next, and nothing be wrong?* He questioned to himself. She balked at his suggestion of counseling, offended at the very notion of it. He was at his wits' end and nearing defeat. Something had to give, though he didn't know what.

He loved her deeply and had hoped to spend the rest of their days together. Kali no longer shared the same dream. Talk of a future wedding was replaced with that of temporary separation. He was determined *not* to let that happen. Her mind was made up and at that moment, devoid of thought. She made a final entry into her journal then placed it on the windowsill. Her golden-brown hair sat perfectly sculpted atop her head. Flawless makeup canvassed her oval face. French tips adorned the fingers of her silken hands. She wore an elegant ivory pencil dress, worn at their first meeting. Her shapely legs rested snugly in a pair of matching heels. The .45 caliber Colt revolver held heavy in her hand.

The morning brought with it elements of confusion and uncertainty. It was a coincidental night of sweet sleep, precipitated by grief and comfort, that thrust them into a place of unfamiliarity. The subconscious drape of their legs across one another's, and innocent lay of Jace's head upon Perry's chest had awakened them in the throes of intimacy. Apprehension and tension between them ensued. Jace had made a hurried exit from Perry's room. Their otherwise ease of conversation was compounded, and the happenstance of innocent physical contact purposely avoided. Words became an instant memory. Jace again offered an iterated apology and nothing more. Perry took comfort in their innocent rest together, while Jace felt threatened by its implied suggestion.

Hoping to rekindle their relationship and avert a possible separation, Asher had planned a weekend getaway at a cabin in the woods for himself and Kali. He was anxious to get home and surprise her with the news. A dozen roses lay on the front seat of the car. He stopped at a local market and ordered their evening meal: grilled salmon on a bed of rice, steamed vegetables, leafy greens, and for dessert, baklava. A bottle of white wine and two candles completed his purchase. The drive home was reflective. The thought of being without her, even temporarily, saddened him. He questioned to himself what had gone wrong, dismissing the thought of her infidelity. The getaway would do them both good. She often spoke of her desire to commune with nature. He thought this the perfect time and hoped it would be a step in the rekindling of their relationship, a last-ditch effort.

Their movements about the apartment were such as to suggest the other was a total stranger. Jace made a conscious effort at avoiding direct eye contact with Perry. Perry indulged him, not wanting to further aggravate the already tense mood. A lingering thought in the back of Jace's mind was the awareness of him waking up in Perry's room, clad only in his underwear, suggesting that at some time during the night he had awakened, and either consciously or subconsciously, disrobed down to his boxers, then got back into Perry's bed, seemingly finding comfort there with him. Their platonic rest together was of no consequence to their friendship, Perry assured him. Jace, not receptive to his words, and decidedly unconvinced, disappeared into his room and gave a swift close of the door behind him.

Turning the corner onto the street where they lived, Asher waved at a neighbor's kid as the boy peddled by on a bicycle. He looked ahead to their home and did not see Kali's car in the driveway. *Great*, he thought to himself, assuming she was not at home but also wondering where she could be. She had always greeted him from work in the past but now things had changed. Her absence would give him time to set up dinner and heighten the surprise. The house was dark and cold, unusual for her to have left it that way, though nothing she did surprised him anymore at this juncture. The current temperature would be disagreeable to her. He adjusted the thermostat to a comfortable seventy-five degrees. Inside the kitchen, he placed the fish, vegetables, and salad on their finest dinnerware and arranged everything *just so* on the dining room table. The dozen roses lay huddled in fanciful wrap and ribbon next to her plate. He dimmed the lights and selected a classical CD, her favorite, then played it on the stereo. The lit candles and soothing music added a warm ambiance and coziness to the room. He stepped back and marveled at his handiwork, smiling in approval. *This should do it*, he affirmed to himself.

Back inside the kitchen, he called her mobile from the house cordless to check her whereabouts, unaware of her presence already inside the home. In the bedroom upstairs, Kali stared at the cell phone as it vibrated on the windowsill alerting her to a caller. Her voice mail answered after three vibrations of the cell phone: *Hi, this is Kali. I'm unavailable to take your call at this time, please leave a message after the beep.* A single tear carved a path from the corner of her eye, down her cheek and over her chin before its short life came to an end, blotting the carpet below. She seldom answered on the first set of rings. Knowing this, Asher hung up and tried the call again. Her greeting returned. The message beep was silenced by a loud explosion that rang throughout the house. *What the...*

Despite repeated reassurances from Perry, the events of the previous evening still weighed heavily upon Jace. Perry's attempts at putting his mind at ease had fallen on deaf ears. He had exhausted his efforts and would not press further. His rationale was that some underlying struggle had been brought to the surface that Jace was fearful of confronting. He could think of no other reason for his deliberate haste and bewildering silence. Jace, suddenly viewing their arrangement as untenable, emerged from his room with a backpack draped over his shoulder and duffle bag in hand. Without a word or explanation of where he was going, he grabbed his keys from the foyer table, and, with a decisive slam of the front door behind him, was gone.

For Perry, the fleeting moment of paradise they shared, now regrettable, had proved disastrous. There was no turning back the hands of time to undo the damage done. The months' long and hopeful bromance that's lived quietly in his head, shattered. Devastated and left all alone—He cried.

Asher dropped the cordless and hurried through the house to locate the origin of the noise. The study and den were undisturbed, as was the living area. A guest bedroom sat ready to welcome its next visitor. The half bath still went unused. He leapt three steps at a time of the spiral staircase that led up to the second floor of the old Victorian home. All appeared to be in order until he arrived at the end of the hall and reached to open the master bedroom door. It was locked. They never locked it. The smell of gunpowder emanated from within. Panicked, he feverishly shook the knob while beating his fist against the recessed door panel. Repeated calls of her name went unanswered. The doorknob, loosened by his aggressive shaking, eventually broke off, making entry almost impossible now. His heart thumped madly against his chest. Delirium skewed his thinking. He became increasingly agitated, while at the same time, predictably somber. His vision became cloudy from the now pooling tears in his eyes. With the wildness of a madman, he forcefully slammed his shoulder against the solid wood door, each blow more excruciating than the one before, until it flew open. Grimacing and wailing in pain, he fell inside at the face of Kali. Her eyes were open and staring directly at him, her lips slightly parted as if to speak. No words were uttered from her mouth. She lay twitching on the floor, blood oozing from her temple. Her perfectly sculpted hair unraveled from the blast. The ivory pencil dress began to spot with blood as her painted face started to smear from the crimson flow. More blood trailed from her mouth and congealed on the berber carpeted floor. Asher, his face awash in a rainfall of tears, raised her up and held her as life slowly exited from her body. His accelerating heartbeat countered her rapidly decreasing one. He cried. The diary, her only voice now, lay open on the windowsill, ready to speak in her stead, ready to reveal its locked secrets. He wiped his eyes and looked down at her. She was barely breathing and soon to depart this life. The classical piece from the stereo played on in a continuous repeat. Her eyes closed. Her breathing ceased. Her heart stopped. The revolver, released from her hand, lay at her side. Miss America was dead.

CHAPTER TWENTY-ONE

The Sound of Silence

It wasn't until the reading of her diary did the truth become known. Asher read it from cover to cover, each page opening a new chapter in her life. Her writings told all and outlined the sordid details that led to her self-inflicted demise. It all made sense now. The diary chronicled her life since the age of thirteen and was sad reading. Born out of wedlock and the product of a broken home, she was destined for a world of instability and uncertainty. Her father, a convicted pedophile and no stranger to local authorities, was absent most of her life. Her mother, supported by the state and addicted to opioid painkillers, was deemed unfit to perform her maternal duties.

He never knew.

There was no other family. She became a ward of the state and was bounced from foster home to foster home.

He didn't know.

There was a time she had been forcibly raped by the man

who gave her life, known only to her—until now.

She hadn't told him.

Attendance to a private catholic school would turn the tides. It taught her well and polished her poise and demeanor. She would carry it into her adulthood. But the scars of her youth would be too damaging to overcome. Though abounding in beauty, charm, and personality, she felt removed from the mainstream of society. Then she met Asher. He was the best thing to have happened to her. With him, there was a sense of normalcy, of belonging. Only kind and loving words filled the pages of him from the read.

Of late, she had become a financial prisoner, swimming in a sea of debt, and drowning; all kept hidden from him. Thousands of dollars were found in her possessions, the alleged payoff from Hutt. Asher had seen the cautioning red flags but could not act upon them fast enough, despite having hired the private investigator. She was in too deep, to the point of no return. His eyes welled up again. He neared the end of her writings and was left agonizing over a passage that seemed a prophetic telling of her death. It was headed *The Sound of Silence*. He read:

> *The sound of silence is what I hear*
> *I walk the road alone*
> *No hand by man nor death I fear*
> *My quest, to make it home*
>
> *Rubber screeched, in the streets*
> *I did not hear a thing*

A shot rang out, a woman's shout
And then the silence sings

The city bustled on and on
And seemed it did not care
Won't someone stop, lend a hand
Help her if you dare

People hurried here and there
As she prepared to go
She said a last and only prayer
They scurried to and fro

To pass the life of one gone on
That's when the church bells ring
A shame to all, yes, everyone
Because they did nothing

She walked her beat in hopes to meet
A paying debonair
To rid their streets is what they seek
It's why they did not care

Why such a waste in this place
I did not understand
A senseless case, I have to face
The apathy of man

I cursed them all upon a whim
Because they brought this shame
But then I see I'm one of them
And equally to blame

Oh, Dear God! Forgive me please
Is it now too late?
I'm just like the rest of these
I helped seal her fate

If had it twice to do again
I'd take a different stance
And not rely on others when
I'd give some hope or chance

I'm almost home, the streets I've roamed
And still I have no fear
The woman gone brings me to moan
I wipe away a tear

My final stop, just one more block
At last, I will be free
Another shot, another drop
The silence sings for me.

He finished reading. It was the final entry in her diary and gave reason for her misanthropic attitude. He pondered the meaning of the passage, its profound words, its telling of impropriety and adversity, its prediction of death. He searched for a symbolic correlation between the woman in the passage and Kali. Was it simply her leisure writing, he wondered, or was the woman of misfortune somehow relative to her? He dried his eyes and read the last lines of the passage again:

Another shot... He could hear the cry of the handgun blasting repeatedly in his ears. He gazed upon her lifeless body lying on the bedroom floor adorned for death. The audible imagery would forever haunt his memory, any instance of silence singing her name in constant reminder. His focus shifted to the revolver lying at her side. It was calling him. The silence was screaming his name.

Another drop... He picked it up. Studied it. Caressed it. Tasted it. He contemplated its beckoning invitation, longing to go with her. Who was this woman he was prepared to spend the rest of his days with—this stranger? He never really knew who she was. He withdrew the revolver from his mouth and laid it back down again. He would not succumb. The silence had been silenced.

The crime scene clean-up crew had come and gone by the time Trudy and the others arrived in Common Wells. Jace had returned from his hurried leave and offered no clue or suggestion as to his previous whereabouts. Perry decided now was not the time to inquire but assumed the obvious—back home. Traces of Kali's remains were nowhere to be found in the bedroom.

Asher, nonetheless, refused to sleep there, opting instead for a motel. He would break the lease on the house and return home to Provident Falls. The funeral home presented him with her ashes that he planned to scatter in the woods where he had arranged their weekend getaway.

Titan/Hutt officials emphatically denied involvement in the garage attack on Mr. Coffey. They deflected attention toward a burglary motive and stood firm in their belief of such, despite the attorney's wallet being found on him.

Maccabeus went on trial for conspiracy to commit murder. Lacking insufficient evidence, he was acquitted. The case against Landon as an accomplice was thrown out. Groundbreaking for the processing plant was slated for next week. Jace and Perry returned to Royalton.

CHAPTER TWENTY-TWO

A Walk in the Park

The papers were in. They were sent by certified mail and addressed to one, Jace Coffey. He did not hear the knock at the front door, announcing their arrival. Perry greeted the delivery driver standing in the doorway and summoned Jace to the foyer. Jace was in the kitchen, making an attempt at dinner. He dried his hands on a nearby towel and went to investigate the need for his presence at the front door. He signed for the documents, then took the nine-by-twelve envelope from the deliveryman. It was a weighty package, and one that would bring an end to his marital union. He retreated to the kitchen and carefully examined the decree for any discrepancies, sifting through all the legal jargon until getting to the matters of importance.

All was in order. Their property was divided as they had agreed, with her getting the bulk of their big-ticket items. All he need do now is sign the copies and the divorce would be final. He patted his shirt pockets for a pen. Perry handed him one from the message cork board by the telephone. Holding the pen in his hand, Jace went into a trance-like state. Perry left him alone to reflect on the years he had spent with his wife. The good times. The bad. More bad than good. The six years he had spent with her were now reduced to that of a stamped piece of paper. A flood of emotions overcame him. He stared blankly into the air. Perry came back into the kitchen. He wondered what Jace was thinking. Had six years of his life been wasted? Was his time with her all for naught. Had she struggled with the signing of the papers, as he did now? Jace sat, glassy-eyed, staring at his very soon-to-be ex-wife's signature, trying to determine her degree of difficulty in signing the document based on her penmanship. He detected no wavering of her signature as it swooped freely across the pages. He was oblivious to Perry having come back in.

"Jace?" Perry softly spoke. Jace acknowledged with a slight turn of his head. Perry walked over to him and, with cautious reservation, began a gentle rub of his neck and shoulders. Jace let out a sigh of relief and became limp as the tension released itself from his body.

"You alright?" Perry asked.

"I guess so," Jace answered, solemnly.

"How about a walk?" Perry suggested.

"That'd be great," Jace agreed.

They walked the course of the jogging trail mostly in silence. The sun shone through the canopy and took on an orange hue as dusk neared. Trees swayed with the breeze. The crisp smell from Lake Royalton penetrated the cool air. Joggers trotted by in their quest for fitness. A rabbit paused to acknowledge them then hopped away. A squirrel scurried up a nearby tree at their approach. Pigeons huddled together waiting for the next toss of bread from a passerby. Ducks from a man-made pond marched in formation to compete with the pigeons. Jace grabbed Perry's arm and led him off the beaten path into a remote section of the adjoining park. They reached an area secluded by trees all around and the canopy overhead, a place Jace had escaped to before, though Perry had never been. Peaceful. Quiet. Serene. Jace led the way as they hiked down a slight depression of the rugged terrain and came to the park boundary, cordoned off by wire fencing and wooden posts. Protected by a shelter of trees and foliage and complete isolation, Jace turned to Perry and looked deeply into his eyes. His stare spoke a thousand words as none were uttered from his mouth. None needed to be said. His eyes told the pursuit of his heart. Perry stood motionless as he gazed back at him, his breathing heavy and heart racing. Still holding his arm, Jace methodically slid his hand down to join Perry's. Their fingers parted then interlocked in a firm hold as their hands united into one. Jace's stare held firm, his eyes granting Perry the key to his soul. Slowly their heads tilted to opposite sides and began to close the gap that separated them. Their eyes closed as their lips made contact. Under a dusk-lit sky, they shared a solitary kiss.

Seconds turned into minutes, minutes into hours. They lost track of all time. Dusk had passed. The walk back was in moonlit darkness. No rabbit to greet them. No breeze to sway the trees. Now, just the occasional chirp of a cricket and distant hoot of an owl in their nocturnal song. The stillness of the night was broken only by the alternating tap of their feet as they met with the earth. Words escaped them. They would be back soon. Jace broke the silence and spoke.

"Your mom was murdered," he said, as a matter of fact, and in a hushed tone. It was as if a ton of cement blocks had been heaved upon Perry's chest. His suspicions were confirmed. He had prepared himself for the worst. Now, having just heard it, was at a loss for emotion. The tone of Jace's voice suggested there was more to the imparting than what was just revealed. He would tell the story. Perry would be a captive audience.

"Did you hear me?" Jace asked him.

"Yeah, I heard you," Perry said, glad that Jace was with him. Their hands separated as the trail led them into a lighted clearing. A few stragglers milled about. They could see the apartments ahead.

The End

EPILOGUE

Jace's room was made into a study that could easily be converted back into a bedroom at a moments notice, if necessary. They weren't sure how his mom or siblings would take the new development and decided to keep it quiet, at least for the time being.

Alex and Jessyca joined a riotous crowd in staunch protest of the impending construction. The contractors, with Titan/Hutt officials, were met by the angry mob, refusing to budge from the groundbreaking site. The police, having prior knowledge of the protest, made their presence known with a show of force and clearly favored the crowd. Maccabeus was jeered as he raised his hands to silence the crowd. Speaking through a megaphone, he made an unexpected announcement, stating that strong community opposition against the project warranted they select another site for the plant. The crowd cheered him, and in a sudden turn of events, he became the hero. Trudy watched the protest and reversal announcement on the evening news, pleased that her late husband's efforts were not in vain. Asher was cast for the television special he had auditioned for, a much needed boost for him. He was soon back to his old self. The nurse aide survived the attack by the now deceased man-boy, but soon after left the profession and also Willie D.

They never heard from the former Mrs. Jace Coffey again.

Rumor had it she became engaged to the 'other' man. Haley and Karter continued calling the two friends in anticipation of another date. Jace and Perry concocted a halfway believable story as to why they could not. Their new life together would relegate them to a world of secrecy, excuses, and half-truths. It didn't matter. They had each other.

www.ingramcontent.com/pod-product-compliance
Lightning Source LLC
Chambersburg PA
CBHW021157010826
48971CB00014B/2722